THE MYSTERY KIDS
Treasure Hunt

h

Hodder
Children's
Books

a division of Hodder Headline plc

Special thanks to Michael Coleman

Copyright © 1995 Ben M. Baglio
Created by Ben M. Baglio
London W6 0HE

First published in Great Britain in 1995
by Hodder Children's Books

A Catalogue record for this book is
available from the British Library

ISBN 0 340 61991 0

Typeset by Hewer Text Composition Services, Edinburgh
Printed and bound in Great Britain by
Cox & Wyman Ltd, Reading, Berks

Hodder Children's Books
A Division of Hodder Headline plc
338 Euston Road
London NW1 3BH

Contents

An unsolved puzzle

'Knock, knock.'

Holly Adams screwed up her nose, closed her eyes, and pretended not to hear. There were times for bad jokes and, as far as she was concerned, this wasn't one of them.

'Come on, come on,' said her best friend, Miranda Hunt, from the other side of the room. 'Knock, knock.'

Holly looked up. She knew she couldn't win. When Miranda was testing jokes for *The Tom-tom*, the lower-school magazine, nothing could stop her. 'Who's there?' she sighed.

'Isadora.'

'Isadora who?'

'Isadora open arounda here? I'm freezing!'

In spite of herself, Holly smiled. 'Miranda, that's terrible.'

'You really think so?'

1

'No,' said Holly. 'I was just being polite. Really, I think it's worse than terrible.'

'Good,' said Miranda. 'It's definitely in then.'

She bent low over the sheet of paper on the coffee table, her corn-coloured hair flopping into her eyes as she wrote. She sat back with a grin. 'Right, that's the jokes column done. How are you getting on, Holly?'

'I'm not,' said Holly.

'How come?'

'Maybe because I keep getting interrupted by someone testing bad jokes on me.'

'Well, they've got to be tested on someone, haven't they?' said Miranda. 'Our magazine has to keep its standards up.'

'Or down, where your jokes are concerned.'

Miranda laughed. It wasn't one of her loudest laughs – they, in Holly's view, would qualify for a place in the *Guinness Book of Records* section on loud noises – but a fairly gentle laugh, doing no more than make the windows rattle.

'So, how *is* the mystery column getting on?' she said.

Holly slumped back in her armchair and

pointed to the blank sheet of paper in front of her. 'There you are. That's it!'

'Oh dear,' said Miranda. 'No ideas?'

Holly shook her head. She'd never had this trouble before.

'Maybe it was a bad idea to try to put together an issue of the magazine for the first week of term,' she said.

'No it wasn't,' said Miranda. 'It was a great idea.'

'You think so?'

'I *know* so.' She waved a hand around the Adams's lounge. 'For one thing your house is more comfortable than the resources room at school . . .'

'Is that all?'

'Of course it isn't. You know what it's like when we go back to school after the holidays – everybody has a face as long as a wet weekend. But with a first-week issue of the magazine in their hands, just think how much happier they'll be!'

'Even with your jokes in it?'

'Especially with my jokes in it! Now, what's the problem with the mystery column?'

'Nothing's happening. Nothing at all.'

3

The idea of the mystery column was to report on the latest mystery books, or on mystery series showing on television. Usually it was a case of Holly having to decide what to leave out. But not today.

'I haven't seen a single new mystery book in the shops,' continued Holly, 'and absolutely everything on television is a repeat. They're even showing *The Man From U.N.C.L.E.* again!'

'I know,' said Miranda. 'My dad says they were repeats when *he* was a kid!'

Holly got to her feet and began to pace up and down. 'What we need,' she said thoughtfully, 'is something *new*.'

'Like my jokes, you mean?' said Miranda.

'*Not* like your jokes,' began Holly. 'My dad says most of your jokes are old enough to have been taken on board by Noah . . .' She stopped, her eyes brightening as an idea came to her. 'Hey! Wait a minute. Why not?' She started pacing up and down the lounge again. 'Yes, why not . . .'

'Excuse me, can anybody join this conversation?' said Miranda. 'Why not what?'

'Why not,' Holly said enthusiastically, 'an *old* mystery? Maybe . . .'

4

'Maybe, maybe?'

'Maybe one that's *never* been solved!'

Miranda nodded approvingly. 'I like it! Hey – how about Jack the Ripper?'

Holly wrinkled her nose. 'For the lower-school magazine?'

'Hmm, perhaps not,' said Miranda.

'But that sort of thing, definitely,' said Holly. She thought a bit more. 'Or maybe even a legend.'

'You mean, something that might or might not be true? Like . . .' Miranda clicked her fingers as she searched for a good example. 'Like King Arthur and Camelot and all that lot?'

'No. Not exactly.'

'Yes, you're probably right,' sniffed Miranda. She gave a sudden laugh, 'Hey! I've just thought – why was Camelot the dumbest place?'

'Huh?'

'Because it was ruled by King Arthur and the Nits of the Round Table!'

'Miranda!' laughed Holly. But she'd got the point. 'OK, forget the legend idea. But an article about an unsolved mystery – that could be really good.'

5

She was still thinking as she drifted out to the kitchen to make another round of milk-shakes. Holly's mother and father both worked during the day, her father as a solicitor and her mother as the assistant manager of a bank. Holly couldn't say she liked the arrangement, but it did mean she could make milk-shakes to her heart's content. She'd just stuck her head into the fridge when the front doorbell rang.

'Miranda!' yelled Holly. 'Could you see who it is, please? And what flavour do you want – strawberry again?'

'Yes, please,' said Miranda as she went to the front door. Then, moments later, she called, 'And chocolate for the paper boy.'

For the paper boy? What is Miranda doing, thought Holly. *Inviting the whole street in for drinks?*

She popped her head out of the kitchen door, just in time to see Miranda returning from the front door followed by a tall, skinny boy with a newspaper bag looped over his shoulder.

'Peter!' said Holly. 'You didn't say you were coming round.'

Peter Hamilton brushed his hair out of his

eyes with one hand, and patted the paper bag with the other.

'I didn't know I'd be delivering the evening papers.'

'*Evening* papers?' said Miranda. She looked at her watch. 'It's only half-past four.'

'They call it the evening edition,' said Peter – the third member of the Mystery Kids. 'Actually there's another edition later in the day, but we don't deliver it.'

Peter smiled. He looked pleased with himself. 'One of the afternoon boys has gone away for the next two weeks, so I'm doing his round as well as my own. It means,' he said excitedly, 'that taking into account what I've saved so far, by the end of this week . . .' He paused to look at Holly, then at Miranda, and then back at Holly again. '. . . I'll have enough money!'

Holly groaned. It had not been a good afternoon. First it had been Miranda's jokes. Then her own lack of ideas for the mystery column. And now Peter's secret. He had been plaguing them with it all through the holidays.

Peter had first said he was saving up for something at the start of the holidays, explaining that he'd taken on a paper round especially for the purpose. But exactly *what* he was saving up for, he wouldn't say.

Since then, Holly and Miranda had tried everything they knew to get him to say what it was. They'd tried persuasion. They'd tried pretending they didn't care (which they certainly did!). Once Holly had said that she would set Jamie on to him, but even the threat of being interrogated by Holly's gruesome little brother hadn't budged Peter's resolve. His secret was still secret.

Once more, she told herself. She'd try once more. 'Have enough money for what, Peter?'

But Peter just smiled. 'I can't tell you – in case they're gone when I get there. But they were there the last time I looked.'

'You want a mystery, Holly?' said Miranda. 'Meet Peter Hamilton, a boy who is a complete mystery!'

Peter laughed, but still said nothing.

Miranda put her hands on Peter's shoulders. 'Peter,' she said sweetly, 'are we, or are we not, the Mystery Kids?'

'Yes, but—'

'Solving mysteries wherever we find them,' said Holly. 'Together.'

'All for one . . .' said Miranda.

'And one for all,' said Holly.

'Yes, but—'

'So secrets between the Mystery Kids are out,' said Miranda softly. 'Agreed?'

Peter nodded. 'Agreed. No secrets.'

'There you are, then!' Miranda said triumphantly.

'And as soon as I get them, I'll tell you. But, if I were to tell you now and then didn't manage to get them, it would be even worse. I'd feel as though I'd let you both down. That would be awful, wouldn't it?'

'It can't be more awful than not knowing what you're on about, can it?' yelled Miranda.

'You'll see,' said Peter. 'All I can say is, they're just what the Mystery Kids need.'

With an exasperated sigh, Holly took the newspaper that Peter was holding and flopped down into an armchair.

'Hey, don't crumple that paper up,' said Peter. 'It's for number seventy-four. You don't have an evening paper from Harry's One-Stop.'

'Then why did you bring us one?' said Holly, rifling through the pages.

'I didn't. I just called in to say hello.'

'Hello,' said Miranda, still miffed. 'Say hello to Peter, Holly.'

'Hello,' Holly said absently.

'Well, that *was* nice wasn't it?' said Miranda. She put her hand in the middle of Peter's back and pushed gently. 'Cheerio, Peter. Do call again.'

'OK, I get the message. But that newspaper . . .'

'Is for number seventy-four,' said Miranda. 'Don't worry, Peter. I'll deliver it for you on my way home.' She looked across at Holly, still with her head in the newspaper. 'If I ever get to go home, that is.'

Peter looked at her questioningly. '*The Tom-tom*,' explained Miranda. 'We've been trying to put an issue together for next week, but there's still a big hole where the mystery column is supposed to be.'

Holly looked up. 'We thought we'd have something about an unsolved mystery. Any ideas?'

'Holly,' said Miranda in mock horror. 'You're asking Peter for ideas? You must be desperate!'

Peter shook his head. 'Not really . . .'

10

'There you are,' said Miranda.

'Unless there's anything on page fifteen,' said Peter, pointing to the newspaper Holly was still flicking through. 'Bottom corner. I haven't had a chance to look at it myself yet.'

Mystified, Holly turned to page fifteen. 'What am I supposed to be looking for?'

'They have a little section on what happened years ago today. Fifty years, twenty-five years—'

He was stopped in his tracks by Holly's shout. Eyes open wide as she looked at the page, she yelled, 'Hey! This could be it!''

As Peter and Miranda gathered round to look, Holly spread the newspaper out on the coffee table. 'Look, look. There!'

' "Ten years ago today . . ." ' Miranda began to read. 'Is that all?'

Holly tapped excitedly at the page with her finger. 'Of course it isn't! Look!'

' ". . . blackmailer Ginger Kane . . ." ' read Peter.

'I couldn't see *that* bit,' said Miranda. 'You had your finger on it.' She bent down to look at the next part of the paragraph, as Peter continued reading.

' ". . . got away with a ransom haul of fifty thousand pounds that had been left in a telephone booth outside Highgate station." '

As he gave a low whistle, Miranda seized her chance to read the next bit.

' "But twenty-five minutes later, Kane was arrested by an off-duty policeman, PC Alan Jenkins, who spotted him and gave chase." Twenty-five minutes later!' exclaimed Miranda. 'Well, *that's* not much of a mystery, is it?'

'No,' said Holly. 'But *this* is.'

She pointed again at the page. There was a simple, final sentence to the paragraph that Miranda hadn't seen.

' "But, by then, Kane had got rid of the money. It has never been found." '

Holly looked at Peter. Peter looked at Miranda. Miranda looked at Holly. They all nodded together.

'Now *there's* a mystery!'

A reference project

'Holly, don't think I'm changing my mind, but . . .'

'But you're changing your mind.'

'No, I'm not,' said Miranda. She swerved across to inspect a pair of boots in a shoe-shop window, then back to Holly without stopping. 'I just don't see how you think we can solve a mystery that's ten years old.'

'I'm not saying we can *solve* it, Miranda,' said Holly. 'Just find out as much about it as we can before term starts. Then I'll write it up for the mystery column.'

The smell of doughnuts wafted out from a baker's shop. Miranda slowed, then hurried to catch up as Holly strode on. 'I take it you're not feeling hungry, then?'

'Miranda, we've just had lunch!'

'We have?'

'At the supermarket?' prompted Holly.

13

'After doing my mum's shopping? That's why we couldn't do this earlier – remember?'

'Of course I remember.' She drew alongside Holly. 'You haven't got anything in your bag, then?'

Holly switched her hold-all from the hand nearest Miranda to the hand furthest away. 'No, I haven't. Well . . . only a couple of cans and some chocolate bars. And they're for afterwards,' she said, switching her hold-all back again as Miranda moved to her other side.

'After we've found out enough for your mystery column? That could take *days*. I could be as pale as a shadow by then.'

Holly laughed. 'You? I don't think so, Miranda.'

They turned a corner. In front of them, at the head of a wide flight of steps, was a large grey building. Even from where they were, they could clearly read the words 'Central Library' carved in the stonework above the entrance.

'So, what sort of information are we looking for?' Miranda asked as they walked towards the library building.

'Anything. Everything. What happened. But especially the route. That's what I really want to know something about.'

'The route. What route?'

'Ginger Kane's route. That little bit in yesterday's newspaper said he was captured twenty-five minutes after the alarm was raised. But in that time he managed to hide a case full of money. So where did he go?'

Miranda stopped, her foot poised on the bottom step of the flight leading up to the library entrance.

'Holly, you're not suggesting we try to *look* for that money?'

'Miranda, what sort of idiot do you take me for? I'm not suggesting that we could find something the police haven't found in ten years. But I have had an idea.'

'Another one? Two in two days?'

'Listen. We could run a mystery column competition!'

'Competition? What sort of competition – Spot the Crook?'

'In a way, yes,' said Holly.

'Huh?'

'We write up all we find out about the Ginger Kane story and include a map of the area, showing the route he took. Then we have a competition for our readers to put an "X" on the map showing where they think the money was hidden!'

'Holly, that's brilliant!' cried Miranda.

'We could have winner's and runner-up's prizes.'

'Right! We could give the winner a free copy of the magazine for the rest of the year.'

'How about the runner-up?'

'*Two* free copies of the magazine?'

'Miranda!'

'Only joking,' said Miranda. 'If we *can* find out something about this it will be the best mystery column ever!'

But Holly was already bounding up the flight of steps and pushing through the revolving door which led into the library.

'Upstairs,' Holly said quietly, pointing to a sign marked 'Reference Section, First Floor'.

'I hope they do keep old newspapers in here,' said Miranda, puffing slightly as they went up the stairs. 'Did you think to check?'

'Peter says they do,' said Holly.

'Oh, well,' said Miranda, 'that's all right

then. If the Newspaper Delivery Operative of the Year says they keep them here, then it must be so.'

As they reached the first floor, Holly wondered if the reference section was actually open for business, it was so quiet. She looked round. A few people were sitting at tables in the middle of the area, silently leafing through large books. A couple were taking notes. A man sneezed, and everybody turned to look at him. Holly wondered if Miranda would be able to survive for long without speaking.

She couldn't. 'Where do we start looking?' said Miranda, much too loudly.

'Over there by the looks of it,' said Holly. A pair of eyes were peering at them from behind a semi-circular desk piled high with books and magazines.

Holly led the way over to the desk. A stencilled sign was perched on the front: 'Reference Librarian – Vera Whittle'. The owner of the peering eyes, presumably Vera Whittle herself, stood up.

'Can I help you?' she said in a hushed voice.

Holly looked at Miranda. 'We – we're

after some – well, information,' began Holly.

'Reference information,' Miranda added helpfully.

'Well, you've come to the right place,' said the librarian with a thin smile. 'What sort of reference information?'

'A newspaper,' said Holly. 'The *Highgate Herald*.'

The librarian pointed over towards a pair of pyramid-shaped racks. 'Today's newspapers are over there,' she said. 'National papers on the left, local papers on the right.'

'Oh. No, thanks – but we don't want to look at today's newspapers.'

'Yesterday's are there, too,' said the librarian. 'I don't store them until they're two days old.'

'You do store them, then?'

'Of course,' sighed the librarian. 'This is a *reference* library, dear.'

'Great!' Miranda said brightly. 'Because that's what she wants, don't you, Holly? To look at an *old Highgate Herald*.'

'How old?'

'Absolutely *ages* old,' said Miranda.

'From ten years ago,' said Holly. 'It's – it's

for a school project we're doing,' she added. For a moment she wondered whether she'd told a lie, then realised she hadn't. It was quite true – the magazine *was* a school project.

The librarian's eyebrows shot up. A faint smile flickered across her face. 'Oh. How nice to see young people interested in the past. But ten years ago . . .'

'You do keep them for that long, don't you?' said Miranda. 'This being a *reference* library and all that.'

'Yes, we do,' said the librarian. 'But newspapers take a lot of space. So most of them are kept in our stack.'

'Stack?'

'Storeroom,' said the librarian. 'Along with the old books. Can you come back on Monday?'

Holly couldn't hide her disappointment. 'Monday? Not today?'

'Stack retrievals take time, dear,' said the librarian. 'I would have to make a special trip to get the newspaper you want.' She waved a hand over the pile of books and magazines on her desk. 'And I've so much work to do I really haven't got time to go again just now.'

She picked up a ball-point pen with her name sellotaped round the stem. 'So, which date are you interested in?'

Holly paused before answering. If it meant going through a performance like this every time, she wanted to be sure that she asked the librarian for the right one.

'Can I look at more than one?'

'*Highgate Herald*s are stored by the week,' said the librarian. 'Six newspapers, Monday to Saturday.' She waited, her pen in the air.

Holly searched through her hold-all and pulled out her notebook. She'd copied out the snippet they'd seen in yesterday's paper. The chase had taken place on Wednesday 26th August, ten years earlier. So she wanted the bundle for that week.

'Week commencing Monday 24th of August,' she said.

The librarian looked up. 'August? You did say August?'

'Please,' said Holly.

The librarian was frowning. Suddenly she slipped from her chair and knelt down on the floor.

'You shouldn't have said "please",' whispered Miranda. 'She's fainted!'

Holly looked over the desk. The librarian hadn't fainted. She was busy shuffling through a shelf under the desk. When she stood up again, she had a small pile of newspapers in her arms.

'*Highgate Herald* for the week commencing Monday 24th August,' she said. Her lips tweaked at the corners in a half-smile as Holly gasped in amazement.

'Really?'

'Yes, really,' said the librarian. She pointed towards a row of glass-panelled booths on the far side of the floor. 'Booth two is free. I suggest you look through them in there.'

Holly took the newspapers. 'Thanks.'

'Very good,' said Miranda. 'Very good indeed. Most impressive.'

'You just happened to be lucky,' said the librarian. 'They were the newspapers I went to get from the stack earlier today. I just haven't had time to put them back yet.'

'Well, thanks anyway,' said Holly, struggling with her notebook, her hold-all and the newspapers. 'Over there did you say?'

'Number two,' said Miranda. She took Holly's hold-all. ''Let's go. You carry the papers, I'll carry the chocolate and drinks.'

'Not in here, you don't.' It was Vera Whittle, looking serious again. 'No eating. No drinking. This is a library, not a cafeteria.'

'A *reference* library,' Miranda muttered as they crossed the floor. 'Oh come on, Holly, let's get on with it. I'm dying of thirst!'

They pushed open the door to the study booth. It was small and cosy, with just a table and two chairs.

'She's not watching us,' said Miranda, looking out to where the librarian had gone back to sorting through the papers on her desk. 'Let's get the cans out, Holly.'

She began to unload Holly's hold-all. Out came the cans of drink, the chocolate bars – and a magnifying glass.

'What's this for?'

'I thought it might come in useful,' said Holly.

'What for, reading the small print?'

'Are we supposed to be investigators or not?' said Holly. She took the magnifying glass from Miranda and laid it carefully on the table.

Miranda thought for a moment, then nodded. 'We are.' She grinned. 'And the first thing I'm going to investigate is one of those cans.'

'No, you're not,' Holly said as Miranda reached across the table.

'Why ever not?'

Holly nodded her head towards the glass panel. 'Because you-know-who is watching.'

Miranda turned round and saw that Vera Whittle was indeed looking straight at them.

'Crafty devil! No wonder she sent us to this one. It's the only study booth she can see straight into!'

With a sigh, Miranda turned to the newspapers Holly had begun to spread out on the table. 'Bit of luck these being around, wasn't it?'

'Was it?' said Holly.

'What else do you call it?' said Miranda, leaning back so that her chair was balancing on its rear legs.

'Suspicious,' said Holly. 'That's what I call it.' She looked at her friend. 'Two people asking for the same papers on the same day?'

'Some coincidence, huh?' said Miranda.

'Papers that are ten years old? Miranda, that's an awfully big coincidence.'

Miranda let her chair fall forward with a thump. 'Of course!'

'Shh!' hissed Holly. Through the glass panel she could see the librarian glaring in their direction.

Miranda looked round, smiled sweetly in the librarian's direction, then turned back again. 'Of course,' she whispered dramatically. 'It's obvious!'

'What's obvious?'

'Call yourself a Mystery Kid, Holly Adams? Use your brain. Who else knew what we were looking for?'

'Peter?'

'Who else?'

It was a good question. Now that it had been suggested to her, Holly couldn't think of anybody else.

'That was kind of him,' said Holly. 'Trying to help.'

'Trying to help? Trying to get here first, more like!' exclaimed Miranda.

'Peter? Why?'

'I don't know,' said Miranda. 'To get his own back, I suppose. Just because we didn't show any interest in his big secret.'

'But we *did* show an interest in his secret,

Miranda. We were dying to find out what he was planning to buy, you know we were.'

'True,' said Miranda. 'Then he's probably tried to beat us to it because we were *too* interested. Boys are like that. You don't know what's going on between their ears.'

'Hmm, maybe,' said Holly. 'Well, let's see what we can find out for ourselves while we're here.'

She picked up the newspaper for Monday, 24th August and laid it aside. She did the same for the paper dated the following day. 'This one,' she said, picking up the next paper in the pile.

'Wednesday, the 26th of August,' said Miranda, scanning the front page. 'Just think. All this happened when I was a teeny-weeny baby.'

'And I bet you were as much of a pain then as you are now,' laughed Holly. She turned over to page two.

'Wouldn't it have been on the front page?' said Miranda. 'A big story like that?'

Holly nodded thoughtfully. 'I would have thought so.' Something that had been said the day before came back to her. 'Maybe this was an early edition for that day. Didn't Peter say that they print more than one edition per day?'

'Something like that. I switch off whenever Peter starts to explain boring things like that.'

Holly flipped over the final page. 'Nothing. The story must have been too late to get in the paper for August the 26th; it must be in Thursday's paper.'

Miranda swept up the top paper from the pile left on the table. 'Good thinking. It must be this one. No,' she said, putting it down again. 'This is Friday the 28th.'

'And this is Saturday the 29th,' said Holly, picking up the remaining newspaper on the table.

She looked at her friend. 'Miranda, it's missing!'

Mystery headline

'You don't think Peter's stolen it?' said Miranda.

Holly shrugged. 'Well, it isn't here . . .'

She looked through the pile again. Monday, Tuesday, Wednesday, Friday, Saturday. But no Thursday. Then she noticed that Friday's edition looked thicker than the others. She peeled open the centre pages of Friday's edition – and there it was. The *Highgate Herald* crest and, above it, the date: Thursday 27th August.

'Good old Peter,' Miranda said as she saw it. 'Can't even stack a few newspapers without getting them mixed up. What on earth's he like on that paper round of his!'

She looked at Holly. 'Hey. What's up?'

'Look,' Holly said simply. 'It wasn't put in there by accident. It was hidden.'

Then Miranda saw why. Apart from the

newspaper's crest, there was hardly anything left of the front page. Most of it had been ripped out.

'That's torn it,' said Miranda. 'Sorry, that wasn't meant to be a joke. It's not funny.'

'No, it isn't,' said Holly. 'Surely Peter wouldn't do this?'

'Who else could it have been?' said Miranda. 'It must have been whoever came here before us, otherwise they would have mentioned it to Eagle-eyes Vera out there. It must have been Peter.'

'I suppose so.' Holly snapped open her notebook angrily. 'It's not right. OK, so tearing the page out was quicker than copying down the details. But it's vandalism. Somebody else might want to look at this paper.'

'Somebody else *did* want to look at this paper,' said Miranda. 'Us! Now look at it. The thing looks like it's been attacked by a runaway shredder.'

The page had been torn out violently, the top corner crumpled as though it had been held in one hand while the rest of the page was being torn out with the other. 'He did it in a hurry,' said Holly. 'He was scared of being caught.'

Miranda glanced out to where the librarian was still sitting. 'Who wouldn't be?' She turned back.

Holly looked closer at the torn page. 'And it was done by a right-handed person. Peter's right-handed . . .'

Miranda blinked. 'Hang on. I've missed a bit. How'd you work that one out?'

'It's been torn from right to left, see? You can only do that if you hold it down with your left hand while you tear it with your right.'

'What if he turned it upside down?' said Miranda.

'Hmm. I hadn't thought of that.' Holly looked down at the ruined front page.

'Anyway, knowing that the culprit is right-handed doesn't narrow it down much!' said Miranda.

'Well, right- or left-handed, he's not left much, has he?' said Holly, annoyed.

Under the newspaper's title, all that remained of the front page was a fragment of a headline and an almost-complete photograph of a man.

Holly picked up her magnifying glass and peered through it. 'Do you think he's one of them?'

29

'Definitely,' said Miranda, moving round to look over her shoulder. 'I mean, look at him. If he's not a crook I'd like to see the picture of somebody who is. Talk about shifty-looking.'

'It doesn't say who it is,' said Holly. 'The caption must be on the part that was torn out.'

Miranda gave the face another close look. The man was thin on top, and looked as if he had recently been in a fight. A short row of stitches ran across his left cheekbone. 'It's got to be Ginger Kane,' Miranda said firmly. 'It can't be anybody else. He probably got that cut resisting arrest.'

'His eyebrows meet in the middle. Isn't that a bad sign?'

'It certainly is! And look at those eyes, Holly!' Miranda moved the magnifying glass out so that the eyes in the photograph expanded like balloons. 'A *blackmailer*'s eyes if ever I saw them.'

Holly looked at her friend with a smile. 'Why, what do a blackmailer's eyes look like?'

'Those!' said Miranda, tapping the picture sharply. She gazed at the remains of the page. 'Not much else though, is there?'

As Holly had said, the page had been torn from right to left. Only a ragged triangular section was left, and most of this was taken up by the photograph. Of the rest, only part of the headline was visible:

Chase ends in Pol

'Chase ends in Pol?' said Holly. 'What would that have been?'

Miranda made a face. ' "Chase ends in Polly the Parrot's cage!" ' She gave a laugh that rattled the windows.

'Sh!' said Holly. Outside the booth, heads rose and the librarian glared daggers in their direction.

Holly looked at the headline again. 'I expect it was something about being chased by the police. "Chase ends in police arrest" or something like that.'

'Hmm, you're probably right,' said Miranda.

'Well, we'll find out when we see Peter. Come on, let's go before you get us thrown out.' Holly folded up the torn newspaper.

As she finished, Miranda took it from her and carefully put it back where they'd found it, hidden inside the Friday edition.

'What are you doing that for?'

'Why do you think?' whispered Miranda. 'Do you want Vera the Vampire to charge us with newspaper vandalism? That would make a good headline, wouldn't it? "Mystery Kid turns into Holly the Ripper." '

'I suppose you're right,' said Holly.

With the Friday edition at the bottom of the pile, they left the study booth and tiptoed back to the librarian's desk.

'Find what you were looking for?' Vera Whittle asked frostily. She gave them a look which clearly said that this part of the library was strictly a laughter-free zone.

'Yes, thank you,' said Holly. Her heart was pounding. They hadn't done anything wrong, and yet she still felt guilty.

'Thank you,' she said again as she handed the newspapers over.

'Sorry about the noise,' added Miranda. She held a hand to her throat and gave a little cough. 'Sore throat.'

The two girls started towards the door. Would they make it? They started walking away. Then they heard the librarian's voice.

'Just a minute.'

Holly's heart missed a beat. The torn

pages. They were in trouble. Slowly, she and Miranda turned round. She knew what was coming. The librarian would be holding up the remnants of the page with the photograph on it . . .

But she wasn't. She had a wintry smile on her face and was holding out something towards Miranda. A tin of cough sweets!

'Have one of these. It might help.'

With a gurgled 'Thanks very much', Miranda took a sweet from Vera Whittle's tin and stuffed it in her mouth.

'And no running!' the librarian called as they disappeared through the door.

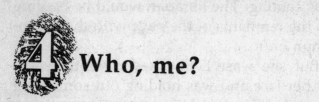

4 Who, me?

Holly strode determinedly up the stairway leading to the flat Peter lived in with his father. It was Monday afternoon.

Behind her, Miranda was having trouble keeping up. 'He's probably not in again,' she called. They'd tried once on Sunday and again that morning.

'He's probably out paper-rounding or whatever they call it,' puffed Miranda. 'I don't know why you don't want to phone him.'

'Because I want to talk to him face-to-face,' said Holly. She checked her watch. Two o'clock. 'And he shouldn't be out yet. His afternoon round doesn't start until half-past four. He said so on Friday.'

As they reached the second-floor landing, she pushed through the swing doors.

'I bet he'll have a good excuse,' said

Miranda, running to catch up.

'He can't have,' snapped Holly.

She was annoyed. Partly because their trip to the library had been a failure, and she'd not found out enough about the Kane story even to get started on a decent mystery column for the school newsletter.

But mostly she was annoyed because of what Peter had done. Stealing anything, even the page of an old newspaper, just wasn't right – especially for a Mystery Kid.

Holly rapped firmly on the door. Peter opened it almost at once. He was clearly feeling very pleased with himself.

'I thought it might be you two,' he said. 'Come in, come in. Have I got a surprise for you!'

'Oh, yes?' said Holly, stepping into the hallway.

'Yes siree! Guess what – I've got it!'

'We know,' Miranda said coolly. She wasn't quite so fussed as Holly about the newspaper-ripping. But for Peter to be a jump ahead of them – now, that *was* unforgivable.

Peter frowned. 'You know? How?'

'We don't reveal our methods,' said Miranda. 'Just accept the fact that we know. Everything!'

35

she added dramatically.

'Yes,' said Holly. 'And we're surprised at you. Aren't we, Miranda?'

'We didn't think you'd go that far, Peter.'

Peter looked at the two girls. 'What do you mean? I did it for the Mystery Kids.'

Holly shook her head. 'Peter, stealing is never right.'

'Stealing?' said Peter, dumbfounded. 'What are you on about, Holly? I earned it. Through sheer hard work. Those newspapers are heavy, you know.'

'Well, one of them isn't quite so heavy now, is it?' said Miranda. 'And we know why, don't we?'

'What?'

'Come on, come on,' said Miranda, closing the door to the flat and waving Peter forward, 'you can show it to us now.'

Shaking his head, Peter led them through the flat and into his small, neat bedroom. Taking a key from his pocket, he started fiddling with the lock on the drawer of his desk.

'Under lock and key, eh?' said Miranda. 'Good thinking, Peter. There are some dishonest people around.'

The drawer slid open. Peter put his hand

in and pulled out a collection of five-pound notes.

It was Holly's turn to look stunned. 'Peter – that's money.'

'Of course it's money,' said Peter. '*My* money. What do you think I've been trying to tell you? I've got it. Enough to buy the surprise I've been talking about!'

'But what about the newspaper?' said Holly.

'Oh, I've still got to deliver *them*. At least until Saturday. But I persuaded Harry at the One-Stop shop to pay me my wages in advance . . .'

'Not *your* newspapers!' exclaimed Miranda. '*The* newspaper! The one in the library.'

'In the library?'

'The one you tore the robbery article out of.'

'Tore? Me? In the library?'

Peter sat down on his bed and looked at them. 'I think you'd better start from the beginning,' he said. 'I haven't been to the library for a week.'

'And you thought I would do a thing like that?' said Peter, after Holly and Miranda had told him about their trip to the library and the discovery of the torn newspaper.

Holly looked at her shoes. 'Sorry, Peter.'

Miranda apologised too. 'It wasn't Holly's fault. She didn't think you would do anything like that. I did.'

'Oh, you did, did you?' said Peter. 'Why? Do I look like a villain?'

'Well, your eyebrows are quite close together,' said Miranda.

Holly couldn't stop herself bursting out laughing. She described the newspaper photograph. Peter laughed too, then.

'He was as shifty looking as they come,' said Miranda. 'And mean with it.' She sucked her teeth. 'Nasty piece of work. That row of stitches . . .'

'Well, at least I haven't got any of them,' said Peter.

'You would have had, if Holly had got hold of you on Saturday morning,' said Miranda. She drew her finger across her throat and let out a blood-curdling groan.

Holly joined in the laughter, happy that they were all back on good terms again. Then she said, 'So if the Newspaper Ripper wasn't you, Peter, and it wasn't us . . . who was it?'

'Mice?' suggested Miranda.

'Miranda,' said Holly, 'be sensible.'

'They do like paper though,' said Peter. 'Harry's had some in the storeroom of the shop. He's going mad. They chewed through some magazines last week before he found out about them.'

'We could go back to the library,' said Holly. 'And ask the librarian for a description of the person who came in before us.'

'Go back and see Vera the Vampire?' Miranda shook her head. 'No way!'

'I'm not sure that would help anyway,' said Peter. 'She wouldn't have known the person's name, would she? And without that, what help would it be?'

'Good thinking, Peter,' said Miranda. 'Forget that idea, Holly.'

Holly sucked the end of her pen. She'd already started a file on the Kane story, sitting up in bed the Friday before to copy out the snippet from the 'Ten years ago today' column. Now she flipped her notebook open and looked at it again.

'Who would want this information – no, who would want the information we *haven't* got?'

'Somebody like us, who saw the article in the paper,' said Peter.

'And is hoping to find the money?' said Holly.

'What we need to work out,' suggested Peter, 'is what that article could have contained.'

'Maybe it would help if we could work out what that headline said,' Miranda suggested.

Holly passed her notes across to Peter. 'Any idea what the rest could say?'

Peter studied the page for a minute. ' "Chase ends in Pol",' he murmured. 'Chase ends in police arrest, I suppose?'

'That's what I thought,' said Holly. 'Which doesn't help.'

'But it doesn't fit the facts,' Miranda pointed out. 'Look. Capital "P". Wouldn't "Chase ends in police arrest" give you a small "p", not a capital? Especially if there's a small "e" in "ends".'

'Miranda could be right, Holly,' said Peter.

'Perhaps we should forget the headline,' said Holly. 'And concentrate on something else.'

'Like what?' said Miranda.

'Like what use that article would have been to somebody wanting to find that missing

40

money.'

Holly racked her brains. What could that article have had in it? What did she put in the articles she wrote? Of course!

'Facts!' she cried.

'What sort of facts? How much money? We know that – fifty thousand pounds.'

Holly read through what she'd written in her notes. 'What don't we know? We know *when* he picked up that money.'

'Five-thirty in the evening,' said Peter. 'Though I don't suppose that's important.'

'What else?'

'We know where he picked it up,' said Miranda. 'Highgate station.'

'But we don't know where Kane was *caught*!' said Holly. 'That's what the newspaper article would have told us!'

'Why is that important?' said Miranda.

'Because by the time he was caught, Kane had got rid of the money.'

'Oh, I get it,' said Miranda. 'If you know where Shifty started and where he ended up . . .'

'You can work out some of the routes he might have taken,' said Holly.

'And where he might have hidden the

41

money?' Peter shook his head. 'I agree. But the police must have done all that ten years ago. It didn't help them find the money though, did it?'

'No. But for somebody starting from scratch, that article would be pretty helpful. It would give them an idea of where to start looking, wouldn't it?' It was a good enough motive for Holly. She pointed her pencil at the other two. 'I think,' she said, 'someone else is looking for that money.'

'Who?'

'Somebody who saw that piece in Friday's paper. Somebody like . . .' Holly thought hard. 'I don't know,' she said finally.

Peter stood up and waved his money. 'Well, even if somebody else is looking for that money, as of this afternoon *we* are going to have something working for us that nobody else will have.'

'We are?' said Miranda.

Peter took the lead. 'Come on, it's time to go. I can't wait any longer.'

'Go? Go where?'

'You'll see. They were still in the window this morning. I checked as I went by. You're going to love them.'

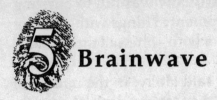

5 Brainwave

'Phew, that's a relief,' said Peter. 'They're still there.'

They were standing outside a small shop. It was at the top end of a narrow lane that until a few minutes ago Holly hadn't even known existed. One minute Peter had been leading the way down the familiar High Street, the next he had turned sharp left, then left again, to bring them to this point.

'Not many people know about this place,' said Peter, as if he'd been reading her thoughts. 'I only found it by accident. That's probably why nobody's snapped them up before now.' He looked away from the window to Holly and Miranda. 'Well – what do you think?'

Holly didn't know what to think, because she couldn't quite work out what it was that Peter was showing them. He seemed to have brought them to a sort of electronics junk shop. The window was full to bursting with bits of equipment. Things with dials, or switches, or bits of wire – often all three – were everywhere.

'Er . . . good!' said Holly. In the middle of the window she'd spotted a pack of cassette tapes. 'Just the thing. They would save a lot of writing. Good thinking, Peter.'

'What?'

'The cassette tapes. We could record interviews.'

'On the cassette recorder we haven't got,' said Miranda, sniffing and looking up and down the lane. A delicious smell of food was coming from somewhere.

'Not those,' said Peter. He pointed into the window. 'Behind them. See – in the blue box.'

Holly looked again. Tucked away behind the cassette tapes she saw the box Peter meant. It seemed to have been in the window for a while.

'Walkie-talkies? You're going to buy a walkie-talkie set?'

'Two-way radios,' corrected Peter. 'But,

yes. That's it. That's the surprise. Good, eh?'

'Brilliant,' groaned Miranda.

Peter tried to ignore her lack of enthusiasm. 'Just think,' he said, 'we can observe suspicious people from different places, and keep in touch with one another.'

'Or carry out investigations and report back to base,' said Holly, beginning to think about the possibilities.

'We can do that already,' said Miranda. 'From one of those glass thingies you see on street corners. What do they call them now? I remember – telephone boxes!'

'But what if we're not near a telephone box?' said Holly.

'Or our suspect is on the move?' said Peter. 'Walkie-talkies let us keep in touch *and* stay on the move.'

'The police wouldn't have them if they weren't useful, would they?' said Holly. 'I think it's a great idea.'

'And it *is* my money,' said Peter, looking determined. 'I earned it. So I'm going to spend it on what I want.'

He pushed open the shop door, causing a loud buzzer to sound.

'Miranda,' said Holly as she went to follow him in, 'Peter's right. They're just what the Mystery Kids need!'

Miranda bit her lip. Peter, and now Holly, were so keen. How could she say she wasn't? Instead, she peered inside the cramped shop and said, 'Look, there isn't room for three of us in there. I'll see you back here, right?'

'Why?' Holly said. 'Where are you going?'

The delightful smell of baking drifted down the lane again. Miranda sniffed the air. She licked her lips, then rubbed her stomach. Now, there was something she *did* need.

'Guess!'

Miranda drifted back down towards the High Street.

Walkie-talkies! It was all right for Peter and Holly. They liked using cameras and computers and all that technology stuff. So did she, really – it was just that technology didn't seem to like her!

At school, things seemed to have a habit of turning themselves off when she wanted them turned on. Or else, when she was absolutely certain she'd turned off whatever it was they were using, suddenly it would start beeping and flashing at her as if it had a mind of its own.

Walkie-talkies! What was wrong with plain old pencils and paper and using your brains?

Like the mystery of that missing newspaper. They had half a headline, didn't they? OK, so she'd joked a bit about 'Chase ends in Pol', but it should be possible to work out something more from that. And a pair of walkie-talkies wouldn't be any help at all.

She twitched her nose. The smell of doughnuts and cinnamon buns was getting stronger.

Forget it, Miranda, she said to herself. *There's a bakery around here somewhere. If you're a detective of any sort at all you'll be able to find it and be back again in a jiffy.*

Back again. Good point. This little turning behind the High Street was a new one to her, too. Reaching the end of the lane, she looked up at the street sign on the corner so that she knew where to come back to.

Pollards Lane.

Miranda walked on. Then stopped. ' "Chase ends in Pol"?' she said aloud.

She stared up at the street sign. Pollards Lane? Could that headline have said, could

47

it possibly have said, 'Chase ends in Pollards Lane'?

Moments later, she had forgotten all about cinnamon buns and was dashing back towards the electronics shop.

In the shop, the deal had been done. The shopkeeper – a short, wrinkled man with wispy grey hair – had already pulled the blue box from the window. Peter almost snatched it from him.

'They are in good working order, aren't they?'

'Perfect working order,' said the shopkeeper. 'Complete with batteries.'

'Really? That's good.'

'An absolute bargain. One of the best we've ever offered in all my years here. Now, if I can explain how they work . . .'

'I think I know,' said Peter.

'I don't, Peter,' said Holly. 'Not really.'

'There's nothing to it.'

The shopkeeper's face wrinkled a little more as he smiled. 'Perhaps I should explain, then.' He looked up briefly as Miranda charged through the door. 'First, the on/off switch . . .'

As the shopkeeper began his explanation, Holly felt a tug on her sleeve. 'Holly! I think I've got it!'

'Hang on, Miranda.'

'Holl – yyy!'

'Hang *on*, Miranda, please! I want to listen to this. It could be important.'

Miranda stood by impatiently while the shopkeeper rambled on about the on/off switch and how to press the 'talk' button when you wanted to talk and how this made the other handset 'pop' so that you knew when to listen.

'Range and frequency?' Peter asked when the shopkeeper finally stopped talking.

A chuckle. 'Don't worry about the frequency. You won't call the police by accident!'

The shopkeeper carried on, not noticing Peter's slightly disappointed look. 'As to range, well . . . that depends a bit on where you are and what's in between the two handsets. Tall buildings don't help. Oh, and they may get a bit crackly if you're near something electrical like a television, or something metal like a radiator.'

'So don't use them while you're sitting on

49

the radiator watching television, Peter,' joked Miranda. She grabbed Holly by the elbow and led her away. '*Now* can I say something?'

'Yes.' Holly looked over to where the wrinkled shopkeeper was still talking to Peter. 'He does go on a bit, doesn't he?'

Miranda came straight to the point. 'Pollards Lane.'

'Sorry?'

'Pollards Lane. This is Pollards Lane. I didn't know there was a Pollards Lane round here.'

'Neither did I,' said Holly. She shrugged. 'So?'

Miranda stood on tiptoe to look straight into Holly's eyes. '*Pollards* Lane. *Pol*-lards Lane. Holly, what if the "Pol" in that headline wasn't the first part of "police" but the first part of . . .'

'Pollards?' said Holly. 'You mean what if it said something like, "Chase ends in Pollards Lane"?'

'Right!'

'Here? In this lane?'

Miranda looked out to the shop's front. Apart from a man wearing a bobble hat walking hurriedly past with a clipboard in his hand, the lane was deathly quiet. 'OK, so it doesn't look like anything's ever happened here. But it *might* have, mightn't it?'

Holly nodded thoughtfully. 'How could we find out?'

'Well,' said Miranda. She nodded towards the shopkeeper. 'We could ask Mr Chatterbox, there. Maybe he was working here then.'

Holly gazed round the shop. Judging from the collection in the window, it certainly looked as though it had been in business for a fair while. And the shopkeeper *had* said that Peter's bargain was one of the best that had been offered in all his years here.

'OK,' she whispered. 'But how?'

'Follow me,' said Miranda. She strode down to the cash desk, talking as she went.

'You know, Holly, I read in the paper the other day about that thing they do in Spain where they let all the bulls out of their pens for the afternoon and let them chase people up and down lanes just like this one.'

The shopkeeper looked up from wrapping the walkie-talkie set. 'Ever get any bulls charging down here?' Miranda asked.

The shopkeeper smiled quietly and shook his head. 'No, nothing too noisy. Usually.'

Holly caught on to the idea. 'How about police chases? Didn't I read somewhere about a chase that ended in Pollards Lane?'

The shopkeeper shook his head again. 'No. Not – well – unless you mean the Kane chase. But that was years ago.'

'Kane?' said Holly. Had they hit the jackpot?

'I think that was his name,' said the shopkeeper, rubbing his chin. 'It was certainly something like that. Dear me, though. What excitement! Oh, I remember it as though it was yesterday. It took me quite some time to get over it, I can tell you.'

'Why, what happened?' asked Miranda. She gave Holly and Peter a look of triumph.

'It was about six o'clock. I'd just closed the shop and was washing out my sandwich box – I'd had salad cream that day, and it had gone everywhere – anyway, then I heard all this shouting going on, so I rushed out to see what was happening.'

'And what *was* happening?' said Holly, wondering if they would ever find out.

'Well, apparently a policeman – don't ask me his name, I'm hopeless at remembering names —'

'Jenkins,' said Holly. 'PC Alan Jenkins.'

'Really? Anyway, this policeman had spotted this chap Kane walking as calm as you like down the High Street. Kane had seen him just in time and dashed off, but he couldn't have known much about the area, because he ran down Pollards Lane, and Pollards Lane goes nowhere . . . well, except to the garages at the back. Anyway, I came out just as the policeman rugby-tackled him. Right outside here! *Right outside!* I saw everything!'

'Any blood?' asked Miranda.

'Miranda,' said Peter. 'You ghoul!'

'Stitches, remember?' said Miranda. 'Above the cheekbone.'

'Blood, you say?' The shopkeeper nodded. 'Funny you should mention that. One of them did have some blood on his face. Which one was it now . . . ?'

'Kane,' said Miranda. 'It must have been Kane.'

'Must it? Anyway . . . the policeman must have called for help – he had a two-way radio just like you've got there, young man,' the shopkeeper said. 'And that was it. Yes, I remember it as if it was yesterday.'

'Kane wasn't carrying a case? You didn't see any money?'

'Money? No, no. That was the big mystery apparently. He'd collected a case stuffed with money. But by the time he got here, he'd dumped it. He wouldn't say where. Even at the trial, if I remember right. That's probably why the judge gave him such a long sentence.'

'Long? How long?' asked Holly.

The shopkeeper shook his head. 'Oh, I can't remember exactly. I remember thinking, "Hmm, that's a long sentence" when I heard about it though.'

'No idea at all?' Holly persisted.

The shopkeeper rubbed his chin. 'Double figures, I'm pretty sure of that. Yes, I remember now. "At least ten years", that's what the judge said he should serve.'

'Ten years?'

A sudden thought struck Holly. All this happened ten years ago . . . and Ginger Kane was sentenced to ten years in jail.

'So,' she said, 'he could be getting out of jail round about now?'

The shopkeeper gave this some thought. 'Hmm. When you put it like that . . . yes. Yes, I suppose he could.'

# 6 Are you receiving?

'MK-one to MK-two. Are you receiving, MK-two? Over.'

Holly pushed in the talk button on the handset she was holding and held it to her mouth.

'MK-two here. Receiving you loud and clear, MK-one. Over.' She turned to Miranda. 'These are *brilliant*!'

Holly held down the talk button again. 'MK-two to MK-one. Can you see anything suspicious?'

Peter's voice crackled back. 'Nothing as yet, MK-two. Can you?'

Miranda leaned over Holly's shoulder. 'Only you, over on the other side of the road, looking as though you're talking to yourself!'

They stopped by a lamppost and looked across the road. A bus came along and stopped to pick up passengers, blocking their view. When it moved off they saw Peter. He'd stopped and was looking across at them. Moments later his voice came through again.

'This is only a test, MK-two. Only a test.'

'The name's Miranda,' said Miranda in a voice that Holly thought might almost be loud enough for Peter to hear without walkie-talkies. 'Miranda. Not MK-two, whatever that's supposed to mean!'

'I explained all that yesterday,' said Peter. 'It's your call sign.'

'MK for Mystery Kids,' said Holly.

'Yes, yes, I heard all that.'

'So when I put out a call to MK-two, you know I'm trying to contact you.'

'Who else is there, then?'

'Nobody, of course.' Peter's crackling voice sounded impatient. 'But that's not the point. It's just the way you do it. The actual call sign isn't important.'

'Then why are you MK-one, and us MK-two? Why can't we be MK-one?'

Peter lost patience. 'How about you being MK-zero, Miranda?'

Miranda put her hands on her hips and

yelled across the road. 'Just watch it, Peter Hamilton! Just watch it!'

Holly took her finger off the talk button so that Peter couldn't hear what she said. 'They're his walkie-talkies, Miranda,' she said. 'So if he wants to be MK-one, he can be MK-one. It doesn't matter, does it?'

'No,' sighed Miranda. 'I suppose not.'

Holly held out the handset. 'Come on. It's your turn.'

Miranda shook her head. 'No, it's all right. You can have my turn.'

Holly didn't need any persuading. Walkie-talkies! Just what *real* undercover teams used! She really felt as though the Mystery Kids were doing things properly now, whispering secret orders and codes that would travel unseen through the air. Even Harriet the Spy would be impressed! Harriet was Holly and Miranda's heroine, even though she only existed in a book.

She pressed the talk button again. 'MK-one?' Holly said into the handset, trying to make her voice crisp and authoritative. 'MK-two calling. Suspicious character spotted. We are following. Repeat, we are following. Keep this line open.'

She veered away across the pavement. Miranda broke into a trot to catch her up. 'What are you on about?'

'It's a test.' She pointed ahead, to where a stout lady with two carrier bags was shoving her way towards a small group of market stalls. 'We're following her.'

Holly spoke into the handset again. 'MK-one, our suspect is wearing a long brown coat and carrying two shopping bags. We are in visual contact. Stand by for further orders.'

'Further orders?' laughed Miranda. 'Peter won't like the sound of *that*!'

But Holly was already ducking between two stalls as the woman put a spurt on.

'It's not a case of orders,' said Holly. 'We're working as a team. This is known as zone surveillance.'

'Zone *what*?'

'Look. Imagine that lady is a secret agent.'

'From the size of her she's more likely to be a double agent,' said Miranda. 'But go on.'

'If one of us follows her everywhere she could get suspicious. But with Peter's walkie-talkies we can share the job. Our zone is on this side of the road, Peter's is on the other side. We watch her here, then when she crosses over, Peter watches her.'

'What if she gets knocked down by a bus halfway across?'

'Then we all watch her! Oh, Miranda! I thought you would be as keen as me about these walkie-talkies.'

'And *I* thought we were going to Highgate station. Remember? We wanted to see where Ginger Kane picked up that case full of money, so that *you* could describe where the chase began in the mystery column.'

'We *are* going to the station,' said Holly. She ducked down the side of a clothes stall as the stout woman turned and looked in their direction. 'But this is *fun*. Come on Miranda, this isn't like you.'

'Right, Holly Adams,' said Miranda, deciding it was time to throw herself into this game. 'You asked for it. Report this lot back to MK-one.'

She ducked down into the middle of a carousel of woolly jumpers, then popped her head out. 'Suspect is feeling produce on fruit stall,' she whispered dramatically. 'Maybe her contact has left something there for her. Maybe it's a plant. No it's not, it's a tomato. She's planting a tomato-shaped bomb! Tell MK-one to clear his side of the street. Emergency! Emergency!'

She swung the carousel round, causing a bobble-hatted man with a clipboard to dodge hurriedly to one side.

'Watch it, stupid!' the man growled as he went by.

'Miranda,' whispered Holly. 'Stop messing about. You nearly ran him over!'

Next to her, Miranda shouted again.

She'd changed roles. Now she was a submarine commander.

'Up periscope,' she cried, bobbing her head above the carousel and swinging round in an arc. 'Battleship on the starboard bow. Tell MK-one to prepare torpedoes!'

She ducked down, then bobbed up again. As she shouted, 'Battleship ahoy! Fire one!' the stout woman with the carrier bags looked their way.

'Fire two!' yelled Miranda, just as the woman finished buying what she wanted and turned away from the stall. 'Come on Holly, what's MK-one doing? Fire two! Holly! Holly! Are you playing this game or not?'

Next to her, Holly seemed to be staring at something.

'Miranda,' she whispered. 'It's him!'

'What?'

'Him! Look!' She pointed beyond the fruit stall.

'There. The man in the grey raincoat. It's him. The face in the paper. The blackmailer. Ginger Kane!'

Miranda stood up in the middle of the carousel. 'Where?'

'There!' pointed Holly. The man was on the move now, weaving between shoppers as he moved towards the main road.

'I don't know,' said Miranda. She formed a pair of pretend binoculars out of her hands and looked through them. As the man briefly turned their way, she put them down again. 'But it could be. It *definitely* could be. He looks older than the man in the picture, though.'

'Well, he would after ten years in jail, wouldn't he?' said Holly. 'You look older than you were ten years ago, don't you?'

'I should hope so,' snorted Miranda. 'Ten years ago I was still in a pushchair.'

The man was almost out of the market area now. Desperately, Holly fumbled for the walkie-talkie handset and pressed the talk button.

'Peter! Peter, are you there?'

'MK-one here. You forgot to use your call-sign, MK-two.'

'Peter, we haven't got time for all that. Listen, this is for real. Kane – the one whose picture was in the newspaper. He must be out of jail. We've just seen him!'

'Where?'

'In the market. He's just leaving, Peter. He's coming your way. Can you see him?'

Peter answered. 'What does he look like? I didn't see the picture, remember.'

'Grey raincoat. Dark hair, thin on top. Can you see him, Peter?'

'No.'

'Then where — '

'Yes! Yes, I see him. You're sure it's him?'

'Definitely.'

'Right. I'm on his tail, MK-two.'

Holly and Miranda looked at each other. Miranda smiled sheepishly. 'OK. So walkie-talkies might have their uses. Let's go!'

Ducking down again, she shoved her way out through the woolly jumpers – and straight into the stallholder.

'Are you buying *one* of them?' he growled, 'or *all* of them?'

Miranda was just about to mutter something about leaving her purse at home when another voice broke into the conversation.

It was the voice of the stout woman with the brown coat. She was holding two carrier bags.

'Oi! Who've you been calling a battleship?'

'I thought we'd *never* get away!' said Holly as they finally convinced the stout lady they hadn't been talking about her. They ran out to the main road.

Miranda looked up and down. 'No sign of him. Or Peter.'

Holly pulled out the walkie-talkie handset and switched it on. Immediately it crackled into life. 'Holly, where have you been?'

'We got sort of held up. I switched off. What's happening, Peter?'

Peter's voice came through. It sounded a little faint. 'I'm following him. He seems to be dodging about a bit.'

Holly pressed the talk button. 'How do you mean?'

'Going into shop doorways. Pretending to look at things in the window.'

'How does he know he's pretending?' asked Miranda. Holly repeated the question.

'Because he doesn't stay long enough to be really looking,' replied Peter. 'He keeps leaning out. Then he checks both ways before moving on. He's doing it now.'

Peter's voice faded for a moment, then came back again. 'He's on the move again.'

'Peter,' said Holly, 'where are you?'

The handset she was holding made a faint sound. She held it closer to her ear. Peter's voice seemed really far away now. 'Peter!' she shouted, holding the talk button down. 'Speak up. I can't hear you!'

She got no answer.

Spot-the-crook

'Flat batteries!' spluttered Jamie. Holly's obnoxious little brother dived behind a chair as she threw a pencil at him.

Out of view, and out of range, he settled down to a game of pretend cosmic soldiers, complete with sound effects.

'It could have happened to anyone,' muttered Peter, looking very sheepish. 'They must have run down while the set was in the shop window.'

Holly made a quick note in the section of her notebook headed General Spying Equipment. 'Remember to carry spare batteries *everywhere*.'

They were settled in armchairs in the sitting-room at Holly's house. Mrs Adams had just come home from work and was busy making something that smelt good in the kitchen. Miranda and Peter had been invited to stay for tea.

'So, what happened after we lost contact with you?' said Holly. She didn't notice that, behind the chair, everything had gone quiet.

'Well,' said Peter, happy for a chance to change the subject, 'I followed him up the High Street. Then he turned right.'

'He didn't see you?'

'No. There was a fair number of people going the same way. They all seemed to be in a hurry.'

Holly looked up from her note-taking. 'He was going to Highgate station, wasn't he?'

Peter looked impressed. 'How did you know?'

'I looked at my watch when the walkie-talkies went dead. It was just about half-past four. The rush hour was just starting.'

'Conclusion – lots of people hurrying towards the tube station on their way home from work,' said Miranda. 'Well done, Holly.'

'Well, as it happens you're right,' said Peter. 'That's where he was going.'

The very place where Kane had collected the money ten years earlier! Holly wrote 'Highgate station' in her notebook and underlined it.

'What happened when he got to the station, Peter?'

'He bought a newspaper and leaned against the wall for a couple of minutes. But it didn't look to me as though he was reading it.'

'Why?'

'He didn't turn the page over once.'

'Maybe he's a slow reader?' suggested Miranda.

'He seemed to be looking over the top of it.'

'Checking that he hadn't been followed?' Holly wondered aloud.

Peter shrugged. 'Then he got his ticket out of his pocket, put it into the automatic barrier and went through.'

'You didn't buy a ticket and follow him, then?'

'I couldn't,' said Peter.

'Why not?'

'By then it was gone half-past four. I was late for my round. Harry's One-Stop isn't that far from the station, so I went straight there.'

'Now then,' said Holly. 'We need to work out what's going on here. Let's go through the facts as we know them.'

She started writing. 'One – ten years ago, a case containing fifty thousand pounds went missing somewhere between Highgate station and Pollards Lane.'

'Two,' said Miranda, 'a couple of days ago a newspaper article about what happened that day was torn out of the library's copy of the *Highgate Herald*.'

'And three,' said Peter, 'you think the man who was pictured in that article . . .'

'Ginger Kane, otherwise known as Shifty,' added Miranda.

'. . . is out of jail and back in Highgate,' continued Peter. 'Don't you think that's a bit of a coincidence?'

Holly nodded thoughtfully. 'It could be. But you heard what Mr Chatterbox at the electronics shop said – Kane was sent to prison for ten years.'

'At least,' said Miranda.

'So, he *could* just have got out.'

'And *could* just have come back to recover the money,' said Miranda.

Holly's eyes lit up. 'Which might explain the torn newspaper. It could have been him who got there before us!'

Peter shook his head. 'That doesn't make sense, Holly. Why would Ginger Kane want to take that piece out of the newspaper? He *knows* where he went that day.'

'But remember what Mr Chatterbox said? Kane couldn't have known much about the area because he ran down Pollards Lane, and Pollards Lane doesn't go anywhere. Maybe he *doesn't* know where he went that day. Maybe he needed the newspaper cutting to find out!'

'And he *was* acting suspiciously when you followed him, wasn't he, Peter?' said Miranda.

'Ye-es,' Peter said uncertainly. 'He did *seem* to be looking out for something . . .'

'Like what's happened to the place where he hid the money!' exclaimed Holly. 'Now *that* would make sense, wouldn't it?'

'Possibly,' said Peter, 'but I'd have said he was acting more like a man looking out for somebody.'

'Makes sense,' said a voice from behind a chair.

As the three of them turned towards the sudden sound, Jamie popped his head out from his hiding-place. They'd completely forgotten about him.

'If he's just been let out, then the police will know, won't they? *And* they'll know that if he wants that money he's got to come and get it, so they'll be looking out for him just in case he does.'

'Jamie,' Holly said automatically, 'you don't know what you're talking about.'

'I do, too,' said Jamie, diving back behind the chair.

'Hang on, Holly,' whispered Miranda. 'Think about it. If the police do know Kane's been let out, then *he'll* know that *they* know, won't he?'

Holly thought about it. 'So,' she said slowly, 'if he has come back then *he'll* be looking out for *them*, too.'

Before they had a chance to discuss this new idea further, Mrs Adams called them to the table.

To Holly's surprise, Mr Adams came through the front door at just that moment.

'Ta-raa!' he proclaimed. 'Diaries and red pens out. Kindly record the fact that today I was home in time for tea.'

'Oh,' said Jamie. 'Does that mean there'll be less for me?'

'I do hope so, Jamie,' said Mr Adams, loosening his tie and sitting down at the table. 'Solicitors need to eat too, you know.'

Mrs Adams sat next to him, with Jamie

70

opposite. Holly, Peter and Miranda sat together at the end of the table. It wasn't until they were well into their second piece of chicken that Holly thought again about what Jamie had said.

'Do you suppose Jamie could be right?' she whispered to Miranda.

'What, about Ginger Kane looking out for the police? I suppose so.'

'It *is* logical,' whispered Peter. 'He would be worried.'

Holly looked at Jamie and shook her head. 'But he's never been right about *anything*.'

'Oh, yes I have!' said Jamie, gulping down a chip so quickly that he broke out in a fit of coughing. Mrs Adams had to rush to the rescue with a glass of water.

'Yes, you have been what?' she said.

'Right,' said Jamie, wiping his eyes. 'About lots of things.'

Mrs Adams looked straight at Holly. 'I know I may regret this but what is Jamie talking about?'

Holly shrugged. 'Has he been out in the sun?'

'They think they've seen a man whose picture was in the paper for doing a robbery years and years ago,' said Jamie with a smirk. 'Ginger Coin or something.'

'Ginger Kane,' said Holly.

'They think he's come back to pick up his loot.'

Mr Adams looked up from his newspaper. 'Holly,' he said in a tone that Holly knew meant business, 'what is going on?'

'We were just testing my new walkie-talkies, Mr Adams,' said Peter.

'And we saw a man. He looked like somebody we'd seen in the paper recently.'

'Ginger Kane? I believe he was released recently. But . . .' Mr Adams sighed patiently. 'What did this man look like?'

'Shifty,' Miranda put in at once. 'Dead shifty.'

'Inadmissible as evidence,' said Mr Adams. 'Conjecture, not fact. Any real detail?'

'Thin on top,' said Peter.

'*Very*,' said Miranda. 'Almost as thin on top as my father.'

'I'm sure he'll thank you for that, Miranda.'

Miranda went pink for the first time Holly could remember. 'Case dismissed,' said Mr Adams.

'Why?' said Holly.

'If that was the man you saw, then it couldn't have been Ginger Kane. How do you think Ginger Kane got his nickname?'

'Not – his hair?' gulped Holly.

'Thick and curly,' said Mr Adams. 'Even after a hundred years in jail, Ginger Kane wouldn't be thin on top.'

'OK,' said Peter, 'so you got it wrong.'

'I suppose so,' said Holly. 'But I was so *certain*.'

'It was a good test of the walkie-talkies, though,' said Peter, trying to look on the bright side.

'It certainly was,' said Miranda.

Peter looked at her in surprise. 'You really think so?'

'Oh, yes. Now you know *exactly* how long the batteries last!'

'Oh, let's not argue,' said Holly.

They sat in silence for a while. They were in Holly's room, the one Jamie-free place in the house.

'Still,' Peter said finally. 'It's a good piece for your mystery column all the same. And I think Holly's idea for the competition is great.'

'Really?' said Holly.

'Yes, really,' said Peter.

Holly brightened. Peter was right. They *could* still use the story. Sitting on her bed, Holly tucked her knees beneath her chin as she thought. 'We could draw a map of the area,' she said, 'and write what we know of what happened.'

'That it started at Highgate station, and ended in Pollards Lane.'

'They could be marked on the map.'

'And that it was all over in twenty-five minutes,' said Miranda. She had moved Holly's bean-bag into the centre of the floor and was curled up in it like a hamster.

' "Use your skill and judgement to decide where the money was hidden. Put your 'X' on the map." '

'Just like those spot-the-ball competitions,' Holly said. 'The winner will be the person who, in the opinion of the judges . . .'

'. . . puts their cross on the exact centre of the loot,' laughed Miranda.

'Well, where the judges think the loot is,' said Holly.

'And who are the judges going to be?' asked Peter.

Holly and Miranda looked at each other, nodded, then looked at Peter. 'Us, of course,' they said together.

'So how are the judges going to decide where the loot is?'

'Er . . . good question.' What Holly liked about Peter was the way he could see what questions needed to be answered. What she *didn't* like about him was the way he asked them!

'We'll have to work it out for ourselves. Is that what you're saying?'

'I'd say you've got to come up with an answer of *some* sort,' said Peter. 'One you can justify. I don't see how you can pick a winner otherwise. To do this properly you're going to have to think like a criminal.'

'No problem,' said Miranda.

'Put ourselves in Kane's position, you mean?' said Holly. 'Imagine that we've just picked up that money?'

Peter nodded. 'Yes. What would you do?'

'Run for it,' said Miranda at once. 'Until I dropped.'

'*I* wouldn't,' said Holly. 'I'd walk. Running would attract too much attention. I'd walk normally.'

'Not with a big beefy rugby-tackling police-man after you, you wouldn't,' said Miranda.

'He wasn't after him at first.'

'Kane didn't know that.'

'All right,' said Holly. 'So I would run until I thought I was safe. *Then* I would walk.'

'With fifty thousand pounds on you?'

Holly lay back on her bed and studied the ceiling. It wasn't easy thinking like a criminal. She knew how she'd felt trying to get out of the library when they hadn't done anything wrong at all! Then something occurred to her. 'He didn't have the money on him all the time, did he?'

'Right,' said Miranda. 'He must have spent some time hiding it. If he was caught after twenty-five minutes, he probably only ran for – how long? Ten minutes? How far can anyone run in ten minutes?'

'Five thousand metres? Maybe more?' suggested Peter. 'That's what they do at the Olympics.'

Miranda snorted. 'Not carrying cases stuffed with money, they don't!'

Holly leaped from her bed and looked at her bookshelf. She pulled out an old *A–Z* of London and found the page which showed the Highgate area. 'How far is it from Highgate station to Pollards Lane?' she said.

Peter took a ruler from Holly's desk and held it to the page. 'Seven centimetres. At a scale of four-and-a-half centimetres to the kilometre that's what?'

Miranda rolled on to the floor and pulled the bean-bag over her head. 'Leave me out when it comes to mental arithmetic.'

'About one-and-a-half kilometres,' said Peter. 'That's assuming he went by the shortest route. Which is due south . . .' He checked the map again – and gave a little gasp of surprise. 'Hey!'

'Hey what?' said Miranda, popping her head out briefly from under the bean-bag, then popping it back again.

'It would have taken him straight past Harry's One-Stop.'

'If it had been there at the time,' said a muffled Miranda. 'Which it wasn't. Becky and Rachel never stop telling me that they had to wheel me for miles in my push-chair to buy me an ice-cream – as if *they* didn't have one, of course!'

Holly smiled. Her brother Jamie was a big enough pain, but at least he was younger than her. She often pitied Miranda in that way. Having twin *older* sisters to boss you about – like she had – must be awful.

'Still, it's a good road to use for the competition solution isn't it?' she said.

A hand stretched out from beneath the bean-bag and stuck up a thumb.

'Good,' said Holly. 'Now all we have to do is decide how far from the station Ginger Kane would have got. Any ideas?'

The bean-bag shook from side to side.

'I have,' said Peter. 'Try it for yourself.'

8 On the trail

'Right,' said Holly. 'Synchronise watches.'

She and Miranda placed their wrists together. 'We are standing outside Highgate station. And it's now . . . ten-thirty-five precisely. Agreed?'

Miranda nodded. 'The things I do for your mystery column,' she said. 'I'll expect you to come up with some good jokes for me next time.'

'You couldn't use *good* jokes,' Holly said with a grin. 'Anyway, you've got the easy bit. You're only walking. I'm the one doing the running.'

'*And* I've got to ride to Pollards Lane, remember,' said Miranda, patting the saddle of her bike. 'Let's hope I don't run into Mr Chatterbox. I'll never get away!'

'If you don't stop nattering you won't even get there,' said Holly. 'Now, are we clear?'

79

Miranda nodded. 'As crystal. I'm going to ride to Pollards Lane.'

'Where Ginger Kane was arrested.'

'The very spot. Then, at eleven o'clock precisely, I'm going to start walking your way.'

'Make sure you do, Miranda. Any riding at all and the test won't be right. And you can remember the route we agreed?'

'Of course I can remember.' She frowned. 'What I can't remember is *why* I'm doing it.'

'Because we know Kane had twenty-five minutes.'

'Right . . .'

'And we're assuming he ran for a while, then hid the money, then walked for a while.'

'Ending up near Pollards Lane.'

'Right. Only we don't know how long he was running, or how long he was walking. We only know that he did it all, and hid the money, in twenty-five minutes.'

'So . . .' Miranda said slowly.

'So, for the purposes of the competition, you're going to do what Kane did, only in reverse.'

'Walk due north from Pollards Lane,' said Miranda.

'While, at the same time, I'm going to start from here and run due south towards you.'

'And where we meet,' cried Miranda, 'is the answer to the mystery column competition! Got it!'

'The winner will be the one who puts their "X" closest to that spot,' said Holly. 'At least we'll be able to say the solution fits the facts of the case.' She looked at her watch. 'Come on then, time you were off.'

Miranda hopped on to her bike. 'I notice Peter found a good excuse to get out of this one.'

Holly laughed. 'Helping Harry set mousetraps in the storeroom of the One-Stop? You have to admit, it's original. Anyway, we'll probably see him. Harry's One-Stop is on our route.'

'I thought he'd earned all the money he needed from his paper round.'

'He forgot about the extra batteries,' said Holly. 'This little job will pay for them. Then we'll be able to use the walkie-talkies again.'

'Really?' Miranda's face fell. 'Holly, do we *have* to use those things?'

'Miranda, of course we do. I can't understand why you don't like them. They work brilliantly.'

'For you, maybe,' said Miranda. 'Not for me.'

Holly laughed as Miranda pedalled off. Just under ten minutes, and it would be eleven o'clock.

She paced up and down outside the station for a while, studying the paving stones beneath her feet. To think Ginger Kane himself had stood on this very spot. It gave her a creepy feeling.

She was pleased with the solution they'd come up with, though. It would make for a really interesting mystery column. And if anybody argued with the answer, she'd be able to say they'd actually tried it.

Holly waited as her watch ticked round. Then, as it flicked over to eleven o'clock exactly, she set off.

Two hundred metres along Archway Road was the first turning they'd decided she would take. It was on the right, heading due south, called Highgate Avenue.

'Ginger Kane would have scooted down a side road as quickly as he could,' Miranda had said when they'd studied the map, and Holly had agreed.

Holly ran down it as fast as she could. In her mind she was trying to imagine that she was being chased by a pack of wolves – which is how she thought Ginger Kane must have felt when he knew he was being chased by the police.

It was this that caused her to miss the next turning. 'Left at Southwood Avenue,' they'd agreed. But Holly was so busy imagining that, instead of going left, she went straight on. Before she knew it, the road had veered sharp right, then right again. She ran on – and found herself at the other end of Southwood Avenue! She'd gone round in a circle!

Annoyed at herself for being so stupid, Holly ran on. She checked her watch. The mistake must have cost her at least two minutes. On she went, back to Archway Road for a short distance, then right into Park Road.

She was back on the route they'd agreed, but as to where she'd meet Miranda now . . . the calculations would be all wrong, surely.

Holly ran on. She'd been going for five minutes now, and was starting to feel tired.

Had Ginger Kane felt the same way? Was it at this point he first thought of hiding the money? She looked at the houses as she went by. They were quite old, all with neat gardens. There couldn't have been a hiding- place anywhere here.

Holly sped on, past one turning after another. Park Road was long, with lots of them. At each, Holly looked quickly for any spot that Ginger Kane himself might have noticed. She saw one boarded-up house. But would that have been empty ten years ago?

Holly was panting hard now. Seven minutes were gone. She was going to have to stop soon anyway, before she collapsed. Up ahead, she saw that Park Road was beginning to swing round to the right. Holly remembered the point from the *A–Z* map. It wasn't too far from here to the High Street.

Where *was* Miranda?

Puffing like a steam train, Holly went past a final turning. Her heart was thumping and her eyes were watering with the effort.

Suddenly, everything seemed to happen at once.

As the road turned to the right, Miranda

almost bumped into her as she came the other way.

And, seconds later, the third member of the Mystery Kids shot out of the alleyway.

'There you are,' whispered Peter. 'At last! Come on!'

Holly didn't even have time to catch her breath before Peter added, 'He's here! The man you saw in the photograph!'

They followed Peter down the alleyway, to a pile of cardboard boxes stacked at the end.

'I saw him when I was in the shop,' said Peter, ducking down behind one of the boxes.

Holly crouched beside him. 'Shop? Where are we, Peter?'

Peter looked at her as though she was mad. 'Where?' He patted the brick wall beside him. '*This* is Harry's One-Stop.' He pointed out towards the roadway. 'And *that*'s Lake Road. It's only short, and runs parallel to Park Road.'

'So this alleyway joins the two together?'

'If you like, yes,' said Peter. 'It runs round behind all the back gardens as well.'

'So where is he?' It was Miranda, crawling

past them on her hands and knees to the very end of the alleyway.

'In that car across the road,' whispered Peter. 'I'd just finished helping Harry set the mouse-traps. I saw him when I came out of the storeroom. He's been there for ages. Just sitting, and making notes.'

'Looks like him,' said Miranda, thoughtfully. 'Shifty.' She looked over her shoulder at Peter. 'What do you think he's making notes about?'

'Which times are quiet, and which aren't. If he stashed the money round here somewhere, he'll be wanting to come back when it's quiet, won't he?'

'But . . .' began Holly. She popped her head above the boxes, then popped it back quickly as a man wearing a bobble hat and carrying a clipboard came out of Harry's One-Stop.

'But what?' said Peter.

'But I thought,' said Holly, as she heard the man with the clipboard walk slowly past the end of the alleyway and off down the road, 'we'd agreed he *couldn't* be Ginger Kane.'

Peering over, round and between the cardboard boxes, they studied the man in the car.

'I mean,' Holly said, 'look at him. His hair's not exactly ginger-coloured.'

'More like black,' said Miranda.

'Disguise,' said Peter. 'It could be a disguise.'

'I suppose so . . .' said Holly. 'Watch out!'

They ducked back in again as, across the road, the car door swung open.

'He may have seen us,' hissed Peter. 'Get ready to run!'

'*You* get ready to run,' said Miranda. 'I'm not going anywhere.'

Behind her cardboard box, Holly watched intently as the man got out. Looking both ways, he strolled across the road. He was coming towards them!

He stepped on to the pavement. He walked to the very edge of the alleyway. He was so close that Holly could almost reach out and touch him. But he hadn't seen them – he was looking away down the road. Heart thumping, she looked up at the side of his face as he moved away. Moments later, the door to Harry's One-Stop clicked open.

Miranda whistled under her breath. 'That was close!'

'But did you see it?' whispered Holly.

'See what?' said Peter.

'The scar above his cheekbone! In the photograph he had a row of stitches in just that spot. It *is* him!'

Peter looked at the two girls. 'So – what do we do now?'

Nobody said a thing for a few moments. Then Miranda got to her feet and picked up her bike.

'How about if I just happen to walk up and pretend to have a look in that shop window?'

'Good idea,' said Peter. 'Harry displays advertising cards in his window. You can look at those.'

Miranda edged out of the alleyway. Whistling tunelessly, she wheeled her bike along the pavement. Then, with a loud cry of, 'Oh, I wonder if my runaway tortoise has been found!' she stopped and pretended to examine the advertisements in the shop window.

Suddenly, she seemed to forget everything and shot back into the alleyway again.

'He's in there!'

'We know that.'

'What I mean is,' gasped Miranda, 'he's in

there *talking*. He was waving a card under Harry's nose and *talking* to him.'

'So – why didn't you stay there?'

'Because I've just had this brilliant idea,' said Miranda. 'Peter, you could go in there with one of the walkie-talkies. You get close to Shifty and press your talk button or whatever you do, and bingo – we can all hear what's being said!'

Peter winced. 'I can't do that.'

'Why not?' said Miranda.

Holly nodded. 'It sounds a good idea to me, Peter.'

Peter looked unhappy. 'Because – I haven't got any new batteries yet.'

'Oh, brilliant!' whispered Miranda.

'I was about to buy them,' said Peter. 'But Harry was having a discussion with that man with a clipboard who came out a while ago. Then, as I was waiting, I saw Ginger Kane outside. So I shot out and hid in this alley. I thought it was better to watch him instead.'

Holly nodded. 'Right, Miranda?'

'I suppose so,' Miranda said grudgingly. 'Go on then, Holly, you go and see what's happening.'

But no sooner had Holly reached the end of the alleyway than she was diving back again.

'He's coming out!'

Moments later, Harry's shop door clicked and the man with the scar walked past. He didn't give them a second glance, just looked hard down the road, then ran across to his car. This time he didn't stay around. He started it up and sped off down the road.

'Well, we can't follow him this time, can we?' said Holly.

'Not unless Miranda wants to pedal after him,' said Peter.

'Not today, thank you.'

'But maybe we can find out what he said to Harry,' said Holly thoughtfully. She eased her way out from behind the stack of boxes. 'Come on, Peter. Let's get your batteries.'

As they pushed through the shop door, Holly still wasn't clear exactly how they could ask Harry what had been said. But she was determined to try if the chance arose.

'Hello, Harry,' said Peter. 'I need four batteries, please. This size.' He held up one of the flat batteries.

'As many as that?' said Miranda. 'I hope they last longer than the other ones. Otherwise your paper-round money won't be lasting long, either.'

The shopkeeper took a pack of four of the correct size batteries from the shelf behind him. As he heard Miranda, he said, 'That reminds me, Peter. Can you get in earlier than usual tomorrow afternoon? I've got a bit of a . . . problem.'

He looked flustered, Holly thought. She nudged Peter in the ribs.

'A problem, Harry?' said Peter. 'Anything I can do to help?'

Harry shook his head. 'No. I just need to get the deliveries over and done with nice and early. That's all.'

Flustered, thought Holly. *He's definitely flustered*. It had to be something to do with what Ginger Kane had said. What was it? And why should he want Peter there early?

'Early closing day, is it?' asked Holly innocently.

As Harry fumbled with Peter's change, Holly sensed she'd said the right thing. Moments later she was certain of it.

'A man . . . er . . . from the council. Just been here,' stammered Harry. 'Told me he needs to close the shop for the weekend.'

Holly and Miranda pricked up their ears as Peter echoed, 'From the council?'

'That's what his card said,' said Harry. 'Needs to look everywhere, he says. In the storeroom, everywhere. See if I need any work done.'

'Work?' said Holly. 'What sort of work?'

'Oh, I don't know,' grumbled Harry. 'Treatment,' he said. 'For dry rot. The houses round here have got it, so he says. And as the shop was built on the foundations of one of them he reckons this place needs to be checked too.'

Still grumbling, Harry put the batteries in a small paper bag and Peter's money in the till. 'Dry rot!' he said. 'I ask you. The shop was only built ten years ago.'

Alarm bells started jangling in Holly's head. 'Ten years?' she said, trying not to look excited. 'Only as long as that?'

Harry nodded. He seemed to be feeling easier. 'I spotted the need, see,' he said proudly. 'A lot of people were moving into this area and there wasn't a general store for them. There was an abandoned house here, so I sank my savings into having it knocked down and this shop built on top of it.'

'Ten years ago?' said Holly again. 'You mean this shop was actually being *built* ten years ago?'

'As near as makes no difference,' said Harry. 'What's the date today?'

'August 26th,' Holly said quickly.

'Well, I opened on the 30th of September. At this time ten years ago – oh, they would have been laying the floorboards.'

'It all fits together!' cried Holly. 'This time it really *does* fit together!'

'It certainly looks like it,' said Peter.

Miranda nodded in agreement. 'Our experiment for the mystery column competition showed that. That shop is only a whisker away from where we ended up, Holly.'

'So, this is how it could have happened,'

Holly began. 'Kane grabs the money and runs for it.'

'He shoots off down the nearest side-road,' said Miranda.

'Just like I did,' said Holly. A thought occurred to her. 'And if he didn't know the area, he probably went round in a circle like I did, too.'

Peter took up the thinking. 'After running for five minutes or so, he's getting worried. And a bit tired . . .'

'Well, I definitely was,' said Holly.

'So,' Peter continued, 'he ducks into that alleyway to get his breath back. And what does he see? Harry's One-Stop, in the middle of being built.'

'He decides to hide the money and come back to get it later. When the heat's off,' said Peter.

'Except that he never gets to come back,' said Miranda. 'Until now, that is.'

'It was early evening,' said Holly. 'All the workers would have gone off home, but the place would have been wide open.'

'No locks on the doors,' said Peter.

'Probably no doors!' said Miranda.

'And with the floorboards only half laid. It

would have taken him no time at all to stash the money.'

'And when the builders came back first thing next morning,' said Peter, 'they'd have carried on laying the floor where they'd left off. By the time anybody turned up to search the place it would have looked as though nothing *could* have been hidden there.'

Holly nodded thoughtfully. 'And now he's back, pretending to be a council inspector. He's going to be let in and given enough time to pull the floorboards up, recover the money . . .'

'And put the floorboards back again!' cried Miranda. 'It will look as though he's never been there. Talk about the perfect crime!'

The three friends looked at one another. They each knew what the others were thinking. Could the Mystery Kids stop Ginger Kane from getting his hands on the ransom money?

'We have to go to the police,' said Miranda. She looked at the other two. 'Don't we?'

Peter shook his head slowly. 'Would they believe us? I mean, they must have searched all over for that money. Would they think we really knew?'

'They would if . . .' Holly paused. 'If we called them just as Ginger Kane was about to find it.'

'What?' said Peter. 'How on earth can we do that?'

'By being there when he does it,' said Holly.

Miranda's mouth fell open. 'There? In that shop? You're barmy!'

'No, I'm not,' said Holly. 'Peter, is there another way into the shop?'

'Ye-es,' said Peter, unsure what Holly was driving at. 'There's the storeroom door. It leads out to the alleyway.'

'Is it locked?'

Peter shrugged. 'I think so. The key's always in the lock, though. It certainly was this morning.'

'Perfect!' said Holly.

'Perfect?' said Miranda. 'Holly, what are you on about?'

Holly explained. 'How about if one of us unlocked that door tomorrow, before Ginger Kane turns up?'

'One of us?' said Miranda. 'One of you, you mean.'

'OK,' said Holly. 'If *I* unlocked that door.'

Peter shook his head. 'How would you get in there without Harry seeing you?'

'You and Miranda would have to create a diversion.'

'What, throw a fit or something?' said Miranda, rolling her eyes.

'Anything. It doesn't matter. I'll unlock the door, let myself out, then lock it up again.'

'Then what?'

'Then we keep watch until Ginger Kane turns up. We give him time to start work. Then one of us—'

'*You*,' Miranda interrupted.

'I,' said Holly, 'let myself in through that door and watch to see what he's doing.'

'What if he hears you?' Miranda objected.

'Miranda, he'll be pulling up floorboards. My dad did that last year and, believe me, it is *not* a quiet job. I can be in and out before he knows it. And *then* we can call the police.'

Peter and Miranda looked at each other, then back at Holly.

'Are you sure?'

'Sure I'm sure,' said Holly. 'Just so long as we can get the key to that storeroom door.'

9 The key

'Are you absolutely sure this is going to work?' whispered Miranda, trying to push herself flat against the wall of the alleyway.

Holly peered over the top of a dustbin. 'Of course it's going to work,' she whispered back. 'What can go wrong?'

Miranda pulled a face. 'I don't know. That's the trouble.'

'If that key is in the basement door like Peter said, then there's no danger.'

'Ah,' said Miranda. 'That's it, then. That's what can go wrong.'

'What?'

'Peter.' Miranda leaned away from the wall and peered round the end. The door to Harry's One-Stop clicked shut as a customer left, clutching a newspaper and a few groceries. 'Shouldn't he be here by now?'

'Yes – *eek!*' Holly stifled a scream as she felt

a hand land on her shoulder.

Holly spun round. 'Peter! Where did you come from?'

'I came through the alleyway from the other end. Sorry, I didn't mean to make you jump.'

'Have you got them?' said Holly.

Peter nodded. Over his shoulder was a bright orange paper-delivery bag. He dipped a hand into the bag and pulled out the walkie-talkies.

'Correction,' groaned Miranda. '*That* is what can go wrong. Them.'

'They've got fresh batteries in,' said Peter.

'Miranda,' said Holly as she clipped one of the handsets to her belt, 'they're perfect for keeping in touch while we're watching out for Ginger Kane. You know they are.'

'Just keep them away from me then,' said Miranda. She bit her lip nervously. 'Are you positively, positively sure this is going to work?'

Holly took a deep breath. 'I'm sure. Come on. It's time to go.'

'I've finished my round, Harry,' said Peter, swinging open the door to the One-Stop.

Behind him, Miranda and Holly drifted in

and began to scan the new arrivals on the magazine rack.

'Good.' Harry checked his watch nervously. 'I . . . er . . . good.' He looked in Holly and Miranda's direction. 'I'll be shutting soon,' he called.

'There was just one thing,' said Peter. 'I put a *Herald* into one house, but I thought they'd cancelled. Can you check?'

Behind the counter, Harry looked at his watch. 'Not now, Peter. Can't it wait until Monday?'

Peter shrugged. 'If you say so. It was number eleven Asquith Crescent, though. . .'

'Oh, no,' groaned Harry. 'I've been arguing with them about their bill all week, you know I have. Oh – just a quick look, then.'

With a sigh, Harry went to the far end of the counter. He bent down to dig out his large newspaper deliveries book.

As he did, Holly slipped quickly past the other end of the counter, through the connecting door and into the storeroom.

The first part of the plan had worked perfectly.

The storeroom was large and gloomy. A

small, barred window of frosted glass let in the only light there was. Holly's heart skipped a beat as she almost knocked over a pile of magazines that she hadn't seen.

She paused, waiting for her eyes to become accustomed to the gloom. Slowly she began to make out shapes round her. More piles of magazines and old newspapers. Cans of this and boxes of that. And more.

It seemed that Harry didn't just use the storeroom for stock. Over on the far side of the room she could see what looked like a collection of ancient office furniture: a filing cabinet, a desk and, in one corner, a large metal cupboard.

Holly moved across to the door. She breathed a sigh of relief.

The key was in the lock!

Murmurings from the shop told her that Harry was still searching for Peter's false cancellation. Slowly, Holly inched her way towards the door.

OK, she told herself. *Unlock the door, take the key, go out, lock the door again. Simple.*

One turn, that was all it would take. Holding her breath, Holly reached out, gripped the key, and turned. It didn't budge!

She tried again. Still the key wouldn't move. The door wouldn't unlock!

Then, suddenly, she heard footsteps outside. Through the frosted glass window she could just make out the shape of a man – a man with a grey raincoat.

She pressed herself against the wall. Who was it?

The man outside was trying to look through the window, bringing his face closer and closer to it as he tried to see through the frosted glass. It was Ginger Kane!

Ducking down low, Holly scuttled beneath the window, round the side of a large cardboard box and then hid behind the old filing cabinet.

She peeped out. The handle of the door was turning. *Thank goodness it's locked*, Holly said to herself.

Moments later, Holly realised why she hadn't been able to unlock that door. It was *already* unlocked.

Before her horrified eyes, the storeroom door swung silently open.

'She should be outside by now,' Miranda hissed in Peter's ear.

'Well, I haven't got any cancellation in here,' said Harry, thumping his newspaper orders book closed.

'Fine. Thanks, Harry,' said Peter.

The shopkeeper checked his watch again. 'Anyway, if there's a problem we'll sort it out another time. Right, now you'd better be on your way.'

He followed them to the door and flipped over the 'OPEN' sign to 'CLOSED'.

'Bye, Harry,' said Peter, following Miranda out.

Harry looked back into the shop. 'Didn't three of you come in?'

'Ah . . . er,' said Miranda, '. . . that was Holly. She – she went out while you were looking in your book.' She hooked her arm round Peter's and pulled hard. 'Byeee!'

'Right,' said Peter, as he and Miranda crossed the road so that they were directly opposite the alleyway. 'Now, it's time for all-round surveillance. Holly should have come out by now. She should be in position at the other end of the alleyway.'

He pulled his walkie-talkie handset from his pocket. 'Now if this doesn't prove to you how useful these are, Miranda, nothing will.'

As Miranda tutted and rolled her eyes, Peter switched on the handset and pressed the talk button. 'MK-one to MK-two. Confirm your position, MK-two. Holly, where are you?'

Holly was in no position to answer.

As the door swung open and Ginger Kane stepped into the storeroom she switched the walkie-talkie handset to OFF. The last thing she wanted was for Peter to be calling her now!

Holly tried to piece things together. What was going on? Why hadn't the storeroom door been locked as Peter had said it would be? Surely if Harry thought Kane was a man from the council, wouldn't he want to show him in himself?

A voice from the other side of the storeroom told her the answer to that question.

'Come on,' she heard Harry say. 'It's all clear.'

She leaned out from her hiding-place as the man in the grey raincoat walked across the storeroom floor. Harry had come in from the shop. 'Where do you want to look?' Holly heard him say. His voice was shaking.

'Over there,' said Kane, pointing to a tall pile of boxes in the far corner of the storeroom. 'I've been waiting a long time for this, you know. Ten long years.'

'You're sure about all this?' Harry said.

'Sure as I can be,' said the man in the raincoat. 'Everything I've found out points to it. And after what you told me yesterday . . .'

Holly had heard enough. Ginger Kane – and Harry. They were in it together!

'She's not answering,' said Peter, staring at the handset.

'I can hear that,' snapped Miranda. 'Or rather I can't hear that.'

'Maybe she's changed the channel setting by accident.'

Peter twiddled with the switch on the front of the handset and tried again.

'Something must have gone wrong,' he said. He looked undecided for a moment, then seemed to make up his mind. 'I'm going round there.'

'Peter!'

'Just to check the storeroom door. She might be stuck or something.'

'What about me?'

'You stay here and keep an eye on the shop. We need to know when Ginger Kane has gone in.'

He started across the road, then came back and handed over his walkie-talkie handset to Miranda. 'Here. Keep trying her.'

'Keep trying her?' As Peter dived across the road and down the alleyway, Miranda looked at the handset in panic. 'How?'

In the storeroom Holly was asking herself what she should do. Wait until they started pulling up floorboards and looking for the money – or try to run for it now?

Suddenly, her mind was made up for her. From outside in the alleyway there came a muffled shout and the sound of scuffling feet. Moments later another man had burst into the storeroom and slammed the door shut.

And he wasn't alone. Held tight in the man's grip was – Peter!

Then a voice shouted. 'Police! Hold it there, Kane!'

It came from the other side of the room. From the man in the grey raincoat!

'No, *you* hold it, Jenkins! One false move and the kid gets hurt. I mean it.'

Jenkins? The man in the grey raincoat – the one they'd been watching all this time – his name was Jenkins?

The snippet from the newspaper. What had it said? 'Kane was arrested by an off-duty policeman. PC Alan Jenkins . . .'

Suddenly, Holly saw it all. Jenkins's picture had been in the paper not because he was Ginger Kane, but because he was the policeman who'd *arrested* him! The Mystery Kids had been following the wrong man – while he had been following . . .

The bobble-hatted man with the clipboard! The man who'd been talking to Harry while Jenkins had been watching from his car. The man Miranda had nearly run over by the woolly jumpers just before they had spotted Jenkins in the market. The man – yes, the bobble-hatted man with the clipboard who'd hurried down Pollards Lane while they were in the electronics shop.

The man Holly was looking at now, who'd grabbed Peter somehow, and was using him as a shield! A man whose bobble hat had been knocked off in the struggle to reveal a thick mass of ginger hair!

Ginger Kane!

'Kane,' said Jenkins, moving towards the man holding Peter, 'I nabbed you once. I'll do it again . . .' He stopped dead as Kane put his free hand into his pocket and pulled out a gun.

'Don't try it, Jenkins, or the kid gets hurt. Now move . . .' He gestured out towards the shop. 'Slowly. This isn't a pea-shooter.'

'Kane, let the kid go.'

'Not until I get what I came for,' said Kane, still holding Peter tight as he followed them across the storeroom. 'Just act sensible, and nobody will get hurt.'

Holly ducked down quickly, almost putting her hand down on a mouse-trap. She heard the snap of a key in a lock. Then footsteps, fading as Ginger Kane led the others out into the front of the shop.

From the shop, she heard the blackmailer barking out orders. 'Empty your pockets. Come on, Jenkins. I know you've got a two-way radio.'

Holly heard the sound of things being put on the shop counter.

'Right. On the floor. Not you, kid. Get one

of those clothes lines, there. Right, now tie 'em up.'

Crawling on all fours, Holly edged out slightly from her hiding-place until she could just see through the connecting door and into the shop. Everybody had their backs to her. Harry and Jenkins, the policeman, were lying face down on the floor behind the counter. Kane had his gun trained on them. Peter, with one of Harry's clothes lines in his hands, was bending down.

'Tie 'em good, kid,' Holly heard Ginger Kane growl. 'Nice and tight. Hands and feet. Good. Now, go sit over there. And don't move a muscle. Or else!'

Holly watched as Peter stood up and walked slowly out of view.

It was her last chance. Any moment now Kane would be coming into the storeroom and starting to rip up floorboards. She'd be discovered for sure. She had to escape, to find Miranda and go for help. All she had to do was unlock the storeroom door and she'd be out into the alleyway before Kane knew it . . .

She looked across at the door – and her heart sank. She wasn't going anywhere.

The lock was empty. Kane had removed the key. She was trapped!

'Come in, Holly! Holly, come in!'

Where was she? Why wasn't she answering?

Miranda twisted the channel knob on the handset and pressed the talk button.

'Come in, Holly!'

And where was Peter? Why hadn't *he* come back?

Miranda pressed the talk button and twiddled the channel knob.

'Come in, Holly!

What was going on? Should she go for help?

But if she did, what would she say? 'My friends are looking for a crook who's looking for some money – we think'?

What on earth was she going to do? *If only I could get some answer out of this wretched walkie-talkie*, she thought. *That would be a start*.

Glaring at the handset, Miranda furiously twiddled the channel selector with one hand while pressing the talk button with the other.

'Holly! Come in, Holly! Oh, Holly, where are you?'

10 Trapped!

Holly was in a jam. She couldn't get out through the storeroom door. And she could hardly run through the shop and get out that way.

Or could she?

From somewhere in the shop came a series of loud thumps, then the sound of splintering wood. Ginger Kane must have started prising up the floorboards in the shop first.

If she could crawl out to the shop door while he wasn't looking . . .

Once again, Holly began to ease herself out from her hiding-place. Further and further, until she was able to stand up.

Slowly, she tiptoed out towards the shop. Nearer and nearer. She needed to know where Kane was. She leaned out slightly – and her eyes met Peter's!

He was sitting on the floor, where Kane

had told him to, his back against the magazine rack.

As Peter's eyes grew wide, Holly put her finger to her lips. The last thing she wanted now was for him to make a sound. Or did she?

Peter's walkie-talkie handset wasn't on his belt. That could only mean one thing. He'd left it with Miranda! Could she get a message to her?

Not by speaking, she couldn't. Even whispering would be too risky. If Ginger Kane heard her, there'd be no way she could escape.

No, she couldn't speak. But Peter could! He could shout something. Kane might shout something back. If Holly pressed the talk button while they were arguing, there was a chance Miranda would hear them and realise what was going on. She'd be able to run for help.

As Peter looked at her, Holly lifted up the handset so he could see it. 'Shout!' she mouthed, hoping desperately that Peter would be able to read her lips.

For a moment Peter looked uncertain. Then he nodded.

'You can't get away with this, Kane!' he yelled.

Holly stuck her thumb up.

Peter yelled again, 'You hear me, Kane? You'll never get away with it!'

'Shaddup, kid!'

Slowly, Holly's thumb moved to the ON/OFF switch.

'How many floorboards are you going to pull up, Kane?' yelled Peter.

'All of them if I have to. That money's round here somewhere. Now—'

Holly flicked the switch to ON. Quickly she moved her thumb to the talk button.

But not quickly enough.

For, before she had the chance to press it, Miranda's voice rang out loud and clear.

'Holly! Where are you, Holly? Oh, I give up!'

At the sound of Miranda's voice, Ginger Kane swung round. As he saw Holly, he started scrambling to his feet.

'Come here, kid. Come here!'

In a blind panic, Holly turned and raced back into the storeroom. Kane chased in after her, the gun in his hand.

'Give me that walkie-talkie, kid. I won't hurt you.'

Holly backed away, holding the handset out in front of her. Kane followed her, crouching like a panther. 'I said, give that to me.'

Holly looked down at the walkie-talkie handset, then back at Kane.

A nasty smile creased the blackmailer's face. 'Give—'

'Here!' screamed Holly.

With all her might she flung the handset at him. Kane ducked, the handset flying past him to smash against the wall.

Holly leaped towards the old office furniture. As Kane lunged after her, she dived under the desk and slid into the small gap behind the large metal cabinet.

Kane's hand reached round, trying to grab her. Holly shrank right back into the corner. Her back bumped against the wall. She could go no further. Any moment now, Kane would have caught her.

As she moved, her foot kicked against something. She looked down and saw one of Peter's mouse-traps.

Kane was pulling at the cabinet, trying to

drag it out. His fingers were reaching round the sides, stretching towards her.

Without hesitating, Holly snatched up the mouse-trap and held it out . . .

The trap snapped against his fingers and Kane reeled backwards with a scream of pain, dropping his gun. A tower of heavy boxes crashed to the ground as he stumbled into them. Kane fell down, groaning.

It was the chance Holly needed. She leaped out from behind the filing cabinet and dashed back into the shop, slamming the connecting door behind her and ramming its bolts into place.

'Holly! Help me!'

It was Peter. In the commotion he'd started to undo the rope round the policeman's hands.

'Quick!' snapped Jenkins. 'Before he gets away.'

'He can't get away,' said Holly. 'The door out to the alleyway is locked . . .'

She realised she was wrong at once. Yes, the door *was* locked. But Kane had the key. He *could* escape!

As the rope binding his ankles fell away,

Jenkins leaped up and unbolted the connecting door.

'Kane!'

It's too late, Holly thought as she saw the door to the alleyway hanging open and heard the sound of running footsteps. *He's gone*.

Then she heard more footsteps and lots of shouting. The sound of scuffles.

Dodging round the mess in the storeroom, Holly and Peter reached the door and looked out into the alleyway. Ginger Kane had been caught. He was on the ground, his arms pinned down by what looked like a dozen policemen.

'How did they get here?' began Holly.

She was interrupted by the wonderfully familiar sound of Miranda's loudest laugh.

Coming along the alley, she was waving the remaining walkie-talkie high in the air.

'Holly, I did it!' she cried. 'It works!'

'Don't ask me how,' said Miranda as they all gathered together in the shop, 'but I just sort of twiddled this and pressed that and was just about to give up . . .'

'We heard you,' Peter said grimly. 'Loud and clear. Trouble was, so did Ginger Kane.'

116

'Ah,' said Miranda, 'but then I heard *you*, Holly. When Kane was chasing you.'

Holly thought back. She'd had the walkie-talkie in her hand all the time.

'You must have had your finger on the talk button,' said Miranda. 'Because I heard it all. "Give me that walkie-talkie, kid," ' Miranda said in the deepest voice she could manage, ' "I won't hurt you." Well, that's when I went for the police.'

'Then? Not before?' Holly looked at her. 'But . . . how did they get here so fast?'

'Well, that was the funny thing,' said Miranda. 'I shot round the corner, and there they were. A whole *vanful* of them!'

As Holly sighed with relief, Peter said, 'Well done, Miranda.'

Miranda shrugged and smiled.

'So Shifty's on his way back to jail, is he?'

Peter nodded. 'It looks like it.' He stopped as a horrified look came over Miranda's face. 'What's the matter?'

'Th-there!' she spluttered, pointing to the shop door. 'Kane! He's coming back!'

Holly and Peter swung round. A man with a grey raincoat was just coming through the shop door.

'Miranda,' said Holly. 'We got it a bit wrong. We weren't following Ginger Kane. We were following the policeman who caught him. PC Alan Jenkins . . .'

'Ex-PC Alan Jenkins,' said the man himself, coming over to them. 'Now Detective Sergeant. You know, it had always bugged me that we'd never been able to find that ransom money. But I fancied Kane would come after it, so as soon as he was released I started watching him.'

'The man with the bobble hat and the clipboard,' said Holly. 'Remember, Miranda? You nearly ran him down in the market that day? *He*'s Ginger Kane.'

'He had to look round for a fair bit,' said Jenkins. 'He didn't know Highgate when he dumped the money, so he had to work out exactly where to come. But when he gave Harry that story about being a council officer, I knew this was the place.'

'So when we saw you talking to Harry – you were arranging to come here and wait for Kane?' asked Holly.

Jenkins nodded. He picked up his walkie-talkie, still on the counter where Ginger Kane had made him dump it. 'And call my men into action as soon as Kane found anything. Trouble was, I didn't get the chance!'

'So that's why they were all sitting there waiting!' said Miranda.

'Yes,' said Jenkins. 'Waiting for a call that would never have come if it hadn't been for you.'

Holly beamed at Peter and Miranda. 'We're a team,' she said.

'Another case solved,' Peter said happily.

'Not quite,' said Jenkins. 'We still have to find the ransom money.'

'Over here, Sarge!'

Jenkins looked over to where a policeman was burrowing under the floorboards that Ginger Kane had been working on.

The policeman had dragged a small, dust-covered case into the open.

As they all gathered round Holly noticed that, apart from a small round hole in one of its corners, the case still looked quite new.

'At last,' said Jenkins.

He bent down and wiped the top of the case with his hand. Then, as he carefully snapped back the catches, he turned to Holly, Peter and Miranda.

'Ready?'

'You bet!'

The three friends craned forward as Jenkins slowly lifted the lid.

'Oh, no!'

'I will never forget it,' said Miranda. 'Never, *ever*. All those mice, just sitting there!'

'In the middle of all that money!' laughed Holly and Peter as they recalled the sight that had greeted them when Detective Sergeant Jenkins had opened the case.

'What was left of it, you mean! All those notes, torn to bits to make a comfy little home. Would you believe it!' Miranda hooted loudly.

'Ginger Kane wouldn't have been able to take it to a bank without arousing suspicion anyway,' said Holly.

Miranda looked seriously at her. 'But it *is* still worth something. All those scraps?'

'That's what my mum says,' nodded Holly. 'So long as there's enough of a banknote left to identify it, then it can be exchanged for a new one.'

'Well, she should know,' said Miranda.

'The end of the paper chase,' said Peter.

'Hey – how about that as the title for your mystery column competition?'

'I like it!' said Holly. 'Except that we can't really have a competition now, can we?' She waved the newspaper that Peter had brought with him. Splashed across the front page were details of the story, complete with pictures and a map. 'I mean, everybody knows the answer now!'

'And who's won the prize?' said Miranda. 'The Mystery Kids!'

Holly looked at her. 'We have?'

Miranda gave a dramatic sigh. 'Holly Adams, don't you ever read the newspapers?'

She spread out that day's *Highgate Herald* on the floor. They all knelt down around it as Miranda pointed to the small paragraph at the end of the story.

'Look. "Ten years ago, a reward was offered for information leading to the recovery of the money," said a spokesman. "As the money was never found, the reward was never paid out. It looks now as though it *will* be." Get that?' cried Miranda. 'A reward! To the Mystery Kids!'

She put on her most serious look. 'What shall we spend it on?'

'How about—' began Peter.

'I know,' groaned Miranda. 'Don't tell me. Another walkie-talkie to take the place of the one Holly smashed trying to brain Ginger Kane.'

Peter shook his head. 'No, you're wrong. I wasn't thinking of another walkie-talkie.'

'You *weren't*?' said Miranda.

'No,' said Peter, breaking into a broad grin. 'I was thinking of another *two* walkie-talkies. That way we could have one each!'

'*Yes!*' cried Holly. 'Peter, that's a brilliant idea!'

'Then we could carry out three-way surveillance,' said Peter. 'Triangulation, they call it . . .'

'And all talk at the same time,' said Holly.

'OK, so the equipment's a bit more complicated, but not too tricky.'

'Oh, we'd get the hang of it, no problem,' said Holly. 'Wouldn't we, Miranda?'

She turned to look at her best friend.

'Miranda? Why are you banging your head on the floor?'